THE

'I've got your number and you leave me cold,' the formidable Karn Fellingham told Jemma contemptuously. Of course he was quite wrong about her—but how could she tell him, now, that she was only pretending to be her worldly sister Christine? Weren't she and Christine in enough trouble already?

THE MAGIC OF HIS KISS

BY
JESSICA STEELE

MILLS & BOON LIMITED
15–16 BROOK'S MEWS
LONDON W1A 1DR

First published 1980
Australian copyright 1980
Philippine copyright 1982
This edition 1982

© Jessica Steele 1980

ISBN 0 263 73890 6

Set in Linotype Plantin 10 on 11½ pt.
01–0582

*Made and printed in Great Britain by
Richard Clay (The Chaucer Press) Ltd,
Bungay Suffolk*

CHAPTER ONE

'YOU'RE not going out are you?' Jemma asked her blonde-haired sister as they stood in the kitchen of Christine's flat attending to the after-lunch washing up, suspecting that when she went it would be the early hours before she returned.

'I thought I would if you have no objection,' Christine replied, bringing home to Jemma that there was a touch of acid about her sister she had never noticed when Christine had lived at home six years ago.

'You have to be up early in the morning to catch that flight,' she reminded her.

'I'll make it, don't worry,' said Christine, relaxing her acid tone, aware that her younger sister by five years was only thinking of her welfare. 'You don't mind being left on your own, do you?'

'Of course not,' Jemma said promptly. 'It was only ...'

'I know, I know. You think if I'm to appear to be young and beautiful before the camera tomorrow I should be going to bed early getting my full eight hours.' Christine grinned, suddenly reminding Jemma of the open-hearted, lovable girl she had been before she had left home to follow her career as a photographic model. 'It's a pity you're here for less than two weeks and that I have this assignment tomorrow, or I'd let you in on a few secrets of what make-up can do for a girl.' She turned to consider her twenty-one-year-old sister. 'You could be a raving beauty yourself,' she said, 'if you used more make-up and had your hair styled and tinted to bring out the red in it.'

'What, me!' Jemma scoffed, having no illusions that

even with the many tips Christine could give her she would come anywhere near to matching her in beauty.

'Yes, you,' Christine said firmly. 'Your features are better than mine, for one thing. And you more than anyone know I didn't start off in life with hair this colour.'

That was true enough. Before Christine had taken to tinting her hair it had been a light mousey colour. 'I wouldn't have the patience you have in keeping it up,' Jemma said with a shrug. 'Besides, I haven't got your ...' she searched for the right word, 'your flair,' she concluded.

Christine nodded as though in agreement, and smiled at her obvious admiration. From there, their conversation drifted to the work Christine did, and as Jemma's fascination showed, Christine let her know her glamorous life wasn't by any means all roses. Jemma knew she had had to work hard to get where she was, and said so.

'The work I can cope with,' said Christine, 'just. But you've no idea what else I have to contend with.' She mentioned the bitchiness of some of the other models towards her, the time spent at hairdressers, and then went on to tell a horrified Jemma of the weird telephone calls she used to receive before she had had her number changed and gone ex-directory.

Jemma was shocked as she told her of the crackpot men who would see her photograph in some magazine or other and used to ring her up to abuse her or make obscene suggestions. She felt the colour drain from her face the more Christine told her, was nauseated that anyone could speak to her lovely sister so, and was not at all sorry when Christine, observing her pale face and horrified eyes, changed the subject.

They were discussing the latest fashions when the door bell went, and Christine broke off what she was saying to state, 'That'll be Mark. Be a love and let him in while I go and attend to my hair.'

Christine's hair looked immaculate, Jemma thought, but she went to let Mark in, knowing better than to tell her so. Quite rightly, she thought, Christine was very particular about her appearance. It wasn't vanity, it was just that she was much photographed and recognised wherever she went, and with the competition so great in the business she was in, she had to take care to look well groomed.

'Hello, green eyes,' said the tall, almost thin young man who stood waiting on the other side of the door.

'Hello yourself,' said Jemma, standing back to allow him into her sister's flat. 'Chris . . .' she paused, almost slipping up and adding the last four letters to Christine's name, only remembering just in time that Christine had underlined to her that she wasn't Christine any more, but was Crystabella. 'Crys won't be long,' she said, inviting Mark to sit down.

'She'll be well worth waiting for,' opined Mark, letting Jemma know if she didn't already that he was absolutely besotted with her sister.

'Have you had a busy morning?' Jemma asked. Mark was a student. She had been surprised on being introduced to him yesterday, because from the snippets she had read of her sister's boy-friends, they had always been much older. Christine had told her Mark was twenty-two. Still, she had liked Mark on sight, and it looked as though her sister was as much in love with him as he was with her.

'I'm always busy,' Mark said grandly, though she knew he was teasing when he said, 'But just between you, me and the gatepost, I had to cut a lecture to get here to see Crystabella.'

'I thought you had exams or something coming up fairly soon,' Jemma said.

'Don't remind me,' he began, then any attention he had for her evaporated into the air as the bedroom door opened and a faultless-looking Christine stood there, pausing for a moment as though to give them time to get the full effect of her flawless complexion and the beauty of her in her white blouson jacket and matching trousers. Mark was out of his chair standing and gazing at her, adoration in his eyes. If it had worried him that he had to cut an important lecture, he now considered it well worth while.

'Darling,' he said on a husky breath, and went towards her, his kiss aimed at her beautifully made up mouth landing on her cheek as she turned her head slightly just before the moment of impact. 'You look gorgeous,' he told her, and would have taken her into his arms had she not moved away from him.

Jemma dropped her eyes away from the pair of them. She was sure Christine was in love with him, but she wished she was more natural. Poor Mark had looked a shade uncomfortable at having this thwarted attempt to take her in his arms witnessed.

'Is anything wrong?' he asked, his natural good humour getting him over the bad moment, his concern more for the light of his life than for his own feelings.

'I'm sorry,' Christine apologised, smiling sweetly up at him. 'I'm still very worried about the lease on this flat, but I shouldn't let it spoil our day.'

'You've heard again from your landlord?' Mark asked, wanting to do all he could to take that worried look from her eyes, but unable to be of much help in this situation.

'No, that's the worrying part,' she told him. 'My lease expires in two months and he's told me he won't renew it.' She sighed, then made what seemed a tremendous effort to cheer up. 'Still, that's my worry, not yours.'

'Your worries are my worries,' he told her solemnly, both of them oblivious to the fact that Jemma was sitting there, though Christine had told her how essential it was she was able to keep the flat on—it was situated in just the right area, and so handy for her getting everywhere, besides the rent she was paying not being as exhorbitant as some of the London properties, and other flats of a similar nature being like gold dust to find. 'Look,' said Mark after a moment, 'shall I ask my uncle if he has anything going?'

'But you don't get on with him, do you?' said Christine, her eyes looking worried again.

'I'll ask him,' said Mark, anything to take that worried look from her eyes. 'And it's not that I don't get on with him exactly, it's just that he's been coming a bit heavy-handed just lately; but that's mainly because my mother has been griping to him because I failed my last exams.'

'Oh,' was all Christine offered, then she sent Mark a smile that had his own smile beaming her way. 'Let's forget my worries for today,' she said, looking into his eyes lovingly, and embarrassing Jemma who because she couldn't stay staring at the vacant chair opposite her for much longer had lifted her eyes at just that moment.

'You don't mind Mark and me leaving you on your own for the rest of the day Jemma?' Christine asked the question she had asked in the kitchen previously. 'I know it's not much fun to be on your own on your holiday, but with me going away tomorrow I shan't see anything of Mark for five whole days.'

She made it sound as though five days was a year, and Jemma was convinced then that her sister must be in love with Mark.

'No, of course not,' she answered. 'It's natural for you to want to spend as much time as you can together.'

'Bless you,' said Mark, touching her hand as he and Christine went to the door, but Jemma had a feeling his comment had been just in passing, his mind more with her lovely sister.

It was quiet in the flat after they had gone. As she had said, she didn't mind being on her own. She had been in London for only two days of her holiday and had a lot of thinking to do, and she was hopeful at the end of it, she would know whether or not she wanted to marry Oliver Davidson.

It should have been simple to decide yes or no; she had been going around exclusively with Oliver now for six months, had thought herself happy in his company. She enjoyed being with him at any rate and doing the things they did. She had enjoyed too his kisses, she remembered, though his lovemaking had never made her feet leave the ground. She pulled herself up sharply there. What had she been hoping for that first time he had kissed her? Had she been waiting for him to set her world on fire? If she had, she had been sorely disappointed, for though she found his kisses pleasant, there had been nothing in them that had made her want to forget herself and go overboard, nothing in his kisses that had her saying, like a couple of her girl friends, 'I just couldn't help myself.' Oliver had rung no bells for her. Would that come, though, if she married him?

Jemma turned her mind away from the physical side of marriage—there was more to marriage than that, surely, despite what the experts said about that side being a good percentage of marriage. In her view experts were confusing. You couldn't pick up the paper without some expert airing his views on something, only to read of another expert in the same field disagreeing with him.

She recalled again the shattered feelings she had had when Oliver had turned to her when he pulled the car up outside her home after they had spent the Saturday evening with some married friends of his. Perhaps it had been because the couple they had visited had been so happy in their domestic bliss it had started off Oliver's feeling of wanting to have something of the same, for he had never so much as breathed the word 'marriage' before, and she certainly hadn't given it a thought.

'Jemma. Dear Jemma,' he had said, and it had been like a bolt from the blue when he had added, 'Will you marry me?'

Her first reaction had been one of embarrassment, she recalled, and she had made an instinctive movement to get out of his arms.

'You will, won't you?' he had pressed, a hint of doubt creeping in, where before there had been assurance, almost as if he thought she had been waiting with bated breath for him to ask that very question.

'I—er—I don't know,' she had got out slowly. 'I—er—haven't thought about—er—marriage.'

'You haven't thought!' Oliver had exclaimed, his voice sounding incredulous. 'Oh, come on, Jemma, surely you must have done. What do you think these last six months have been leading up to if not that?'

'I hadn't thought about marriage,' she had confessed, which was true. Oliver was good company, pleasant to go out with, not demanding in his lovemaking.

'Well, surely to God you didn't think I was leading up to asking you to live with me without marriage, did you?'

'Live with you without ...!' she had gasped, such a thought never having entered her head.

'That's not what I want either,' Oliver had said, rather pompously she had thought, as though had that been in his mind she would have agreed more readily. 'Don't play hard to get, Jemma, it's not like you to prevaricate. I've got a good job at the bank. The bank will let me have a mortgage at a reduced rate of interest, and although you'll have to keep on with your job for a while, in about three years we should have a comfortable home about us, then you can leave work and we can start a family.'

A home, a mortgage, a family! Jemma had experienced panic. She was conscious of being rushed, conscious of something in her that said at twenty-one and a half she

wouldn't have minded if life had a few surprises for her—
a feeling she had had once or twice recently, she had to
admit—but the surprise Oliver had just sprung on her was
one surprise she hadn't been ready for. Her panic helped
her in extricating herself from his arms.

'I don't know, Oliver,' she had said quickly, aware in
the darkness of the car that he would be frowning at her.
It sounded trite to say, 'This is so sudden', but it was, and
she knew herself floundering.

'What don't you know?' he had asked. 'You enjoy going
out with me, enjoy my company as I enjoy yours. We like
the same things, our minds are always in tune about
absolutely everything. And physically we're suited, aren't
we? You like it when I kiss you, don't you?'

'Yes,' she had to confess. She had enjoyed his brand of
kisses, enjoyed experimenting on the edge of physical pleasure, though his lovemaking had always stopped when he
had discovered she was prepared to let him kiss her but no
more.

Oliver hadn't wanted to let her go in until she had
given him the answer he wanted, but the suddenness of his
proposal had so confused her, she had no idea what she
wanted other than that something inside her was telling
her that marriage for her had to be a once-in-a-lifetime
thing, and until she was sure that marriage to Oliver was
what she wanted, then she just couldn't give him her promise, not until she had thought the matter over.

Vaguely she was aware that if she loved him enough to
marry him she wouldn't have to think about it at all. Then
she remembered she had always thought herself happy
with him, and her confusion grew larger. Reluctantly he
had let her go into the house where she lived with her
parents, his proposal unanswered. She had said she would
give him his answer when she saw him again, which because he was playing an away game of cricket tomorrow

and had night school on Monday, would be next Tuesday.

It seemed to Jemma she had lain awake most of the night trying to picture herself married to Oliver, but she must have gone to sleep at some stage, for her mother calling, 'Jemma, it's about time you were up!' had her surfacing to realise Sunday morning was about to get under way, but had brought with it no clear picture of her as Oliver's wife.

All through that day she fretted at the question, even at one point turning against Oliver for having asked the question and spoiling what had been a comfortable friendship, before she realised it must have looked to him as though she was willing to be his bride since she had had no other boy-friends since she had started going out with him. No mention had been made of love in his proposal, yet he must love her, mustn't he? But did she love him? She just didn't know. And suddenly Tuesday, the day he would expect his answer, seemed much to close, and she experienced an alarming sensation of panic that if Oliver badgered at her the way he had last night, she just might not find the courage to tell him if her answer was 'No'.

At tea time that Sunday her mother asked her if anything was the matter. 'You've been very quiet all day,' she observed.

'Probably had a row with Oliver,' said her father, who was the dearest man and the biggest tease.

'Have you had a row with Oliver?' her mother asked in her forthright manner.

'No, nothing like that,' Jemma said quickly.

'Well, something's bothering you.'

'I was thinking of going away for a while.' The statement left her lips without her being aware the idea had been formed, but as the idea grew in her mind, for the first time that day she felt her spirits lifting, and as she saw she had the attention of both her mother and father she found herself adding, 'Mr Riley is still away from the office on sick leave; it wouldn't inconvenience anybody if I took two weeks off. I could go and stay with Christine in London.'

At the mention of her sister's name her mother was all for the idea. Christine seldom came home at all these days, if Jemma went she could bring home all the news of Christine's happenings, and since Jemma was a good little cook, she would see to it that her sister had some decent food inside her. The last time Christine had been home she had let it slip that if she felt hungry she usually boiled something in a plastic bag for twenty or so minutes.

Things were slack at the office and Jemma had no trouble in getting the time off when she had gone to work the next day, and it was agreed she could start her annual holiday from the following morning. She had been fortunate too when ringing Christine to find her in and welcoming her visit. Jemma had a few qualms when it came to ringing Oliver, as in all fairness she had to, and it wasn't helped any by his eager-sounding:

'Ah, Jemma—you couldn't wait until tomorrow night to tell me your answer.'

She knew then that her decision to go away was the right one. Oliver obviously expected her answer to be 'Yes' and she couldn't yet face him if her answer was to be 'No'. He hadn't liked it when she had said she was going away for almost a fortnight, had wanted to come round and see her that night when he had finished his class, and had shown a sulky side to his nature she had never noticed before when she had said she would rather he didn't because she had no answer for him.

The sound of someone ringing Christine's door bell had Jemma leaving her thoughts and getting to her feet. She had a smile on her face ready to explain if the caller was a friend of Christine's, that her sister was out, but that she would be pleased to take a message.

Her smile quickly faded when on pulling back the door she saw a grim-faced man standing there. He was tall and dark-haired, and just one look at his unfriendly expression told her he was no friend of her sister's—a friend of very few other people either, if she was any judge.

'Yes?' she enquired, and was about to ask what he wanted when from nowhere the remembrance of Christine telling her of the odd-ball telephone calls she used to get shot into her head, and she felt her insides begin to tremble.

The man didn't answer her 'Yes?' and the suspicion began to grow, as he looked her over with a scrutiny that could only be called insolent, that since Christine was now ex-directory this man had called in person to abuse her sister, and would soon tell her in no uncertain language what he wanted.

Her reflexes tensed ready to slam the door in his face as the suspicion became conviction, the longer he continued his inspection of her, that he *was* one of the type Christine had told her about. And then he spoke.

'Do I have the *pleasure* of addressing Miss Crystabella Nokes?' he asked. His voice, deep and cultured, was about the only nice thing about him, she thought, and her suspicions about him dipped briefly as she reasoned that he couldn't have seen a picture of her blonde sister or he would know she couldn't be her.

Then her mind reasoned that he could well think with his disturbed thoughts that she wore a blonde wig for her job, and with make-up ... Then the sneering way he had said 'pleasure' hit her, and she became more certain than ever that he had come here with some idea of harming Christine.

Why she just didn't slam the door on him then and there Jemma didn't know. Maybe because there was some undefined idea in the back of her mind that if she could get rid of him amicably, then he would not at some later date return to pester her sister.

'And if I am Crystabella Nokes?' she asked, feeling some surprise that she had managed to make her voice sound coolly interested, when she had thought it would have come out as reedy and shaking as her insides felt.

'Then you and I have some business to transact,' he replied, obviously gathering from her answer that she was indeed Crystabella Nokes.

'Oh?' said Jemma, making her voice sound just a shade curious. No point in antagonising him. But it was clear since he had had to ask who she was that he had never met Christine, and if she had anything to do with it, he wasn't going to.

'Do you usually conduct your business at your door?' he asked.

His grim expression had not lightened since she had opened the door, but if he thought he was going to gain entry into Christine's flat by some ploy of having business with her, then he could think again.

'My name is Karn Fellingham,' he added, and said it as if he expected her to know who he was, so that for a moment she wondered if she had made a mistake.

She couldn't quite shrug the thought away, because it was just possible that he could be someone who had some work for Christine. Though wouldn't he have gone to her agent rather than make a direct approach?

'My agent handles all my business,' she said, hoping she wasn't in the act of losing Christine a contract, but sure, or ninety-nine per cent sure, that her instinct was right when it told her this man's presence here boded nothing but ill for her sister.

Karn Fellingham ignored her comment. 'My nephew has obviously not mentioned my name,' he said, beginning to sound bored that he was on her doorstep at all.

Nephew! 'Oh,' said Jemma, and 'Oh', again as she remembered Mark had mentioned an uncle less than an hour
ago and how he was going to approach his uncle about the
possibility of him having a flat available for Christine to
rent. Oh, my giddy aunt! she thought; far from being a
man out to harm her sister, if he was Mark's uncle he could
well be the man who had the answer to Christine's very
pressing worry of the moment. But first she had to be sure.
Her tendency to be too quick with her conclusions before
she had time to think had just tripped her up—or had it?

'You're ...?'

'Mark Stevens' uncle,' he confirmed shortly.

Jemma felt all sorts of a fool, though she hoped it wasn't
showing, as she stood back from the door and belatedly
invited him in.

Karn Fellingham came in, his head just missing the top
of the door as he did so. Jemma had always been aware of
her own five feet eight inches, but she felt dwarfed by this
tall, broad-shouldered man.

Once inside the room where the light was better, she
saw the straight dark hair, cut short but with a swathe that
threatened to fall over his forehead, was liberally sprinkled
with grey at the temples, giving his grim countenance a
distinguished look. Realising she had better get started
straight away on telling him she was Jemma, not Crystabella, she opened her mouth, only to close it again when
Karn Fellingham gave her a look she read as saying he was
impatient to be gone, followed by a terse:

'I won't take up more than a minute of your time, Miss
Nokes. I've called purely to tell you to keep your claws
away from my nephew and allow him to get on with his
studies.'

His insolent arrogance stunned her for seconds, and she
could only stare at him open-mouthed. All thoughts of telling him her true identity vanished. She just couldn't credit

what she was hearing. That a man she had never before met, a man who had never met her lovely sister, could calmly walk in and try to dictate to her that Christine should keep her claws out of ...

'*Claws!*' she gasped at last, that one word isolating itself from the others.

'Claws, Miss Nokes,' he repeated, not backing down one iota at her astonishment. 'Cut out the big act and heed what I say. Finish whatever it is you have going between you and Mark and leave him to get on with some work.'

'Finish?' Jemma whispered, then as anger started to well up within her, and with it the knowledge that she hadn't jumped to the wrong conclusion when thinking that this man boded ill for Christine, she had to hang on not to let her anger have its head.

No, she mustn't give way to the rage that was rising to boiling point within her, she thought, trying to quell her fury as she reasoned that if she kept her temper in check then she might be able to do more for her sister's cause than if she let fly. Christine would never forgive her, rightly so, if instead of trying to help her she drove a deep wedge into any future relationship she might have with Mark's family.

'Have you never heard of true love, Mr Fellingham?' she managed, after much difficulty, keeping the heat out of her voice and about to add who she was, and then try to impress on him how very much in love with Mark her sister was.

But before she could say more he was favouring her with a look from down his nose it would take her years to learn to imitate. Then astoundingly, while she could only clutch on to the back of the chair in front of her, so great was her amazement, his hand went to his inside pocket and he withdrew his cheque book.

'Love!' he sneered. 'What do you know of love? I've

heard about you, Crystabella Nokes. You wouldn't know love if you were hit on the head with it; not unless it had a pound sign in front of it.' He turned his back to her, taking out his pen and seating himself in front of the occasional table. 'How much?' he asked shortly, looking all set to write out a cheque for the amount he thought would buy off Crystabella Nokes, and missed entirely the look of outrage that passed over Jemma's face.

Fury like no other she had ever experienced stormed through her as she watched him open his cheque book and write Nokes on the counterfoil. It was written in a firm black handwriting, and in that second it took him to write, Jemma's fury had turned into ice-cold anger, and any thoughts she had had on trying to help Christine's cause went scurrying.

'Don't be shy, Miss Nokes,' he instructed her, 'I'm sure you're not unused to this situation. What's your usual fee?'

'Five thousand,' said Jemma tightly, and waited to hurl invective at him when he argued against the figure.

'You do sell yourself high,' he said, not turning a hair. 'But then it would be cheap at twice the price to get him away from the likes of you.'

How she stopped her hand from whipping down and clouting the back of his head, Jemma didn't know. But with her hands gripped tightly behind her, she stood and watched him fill in the cheque and sign it, leaving only the space for her name blank.

'What's your real name?' he asked, his pen poised, not even bothering to look at her.

'Real name?' Jemma hedged, unsure now whether she wanted him to know she wasn't Christine, but thinking from his question that he had somehow guessed, though why he was still set on writing that cheque ...

'It's unlikely you were labelled Crystabella when you

were born,' he said, too ready in her opinion with his pronouncements.

And then, still ice-cold with anger, she realised that what was happening was between her and Karn Fellingham alone. Christine didn't figure in it anywhere at all just then, and it was going to be Jemma Nokes who was going to have the glorious satisfaction of tearing up his cheque and ...

'Well?' he said with short impatience.

'Jemma,' she told him, barely able to wait to get her hands on the cheque so she could turn the tables on him. 'My name is Jemma Nokes.'

Seconds later she was looking up into the hardest brown eyes she had ever seen, as he stood up and thrust the cheque into her hands.

'Right, Jemma Nokes,' he said, capping his fountain pen and preparing to leave. 'I don't give a damn what you tell my nephew, but the account is squared my end. You cut him out of your life from here on.' He paused, and while Jemma was savouring that the moment was almost here when she could have her turn, he added, 'Try double-crossing me, Jemma Nokes, and you'll live to regret it.'

Then to her astonishment, before she could carry through her intention of ripping his cheque into small pieces and stuffing them into his top pocket with a few well chosen and if possible cutting words, Karn Fellingham had turned sharply, and as if he found the distaste of breathing the same air as her too much, he strode from the room.

How long she stood and just stared at that closed door, Jemma couldn't have said. But the longer she just stood and stared, the more unreal the scene she had been part of seemed to be. It was utterly fantastic that Mark's uncle had coldly sat on that settee over there filling in a cheque as though he had better things to do with his time than to visit his nephew's girl-friends and 'square accounts' with them. Yet she was still clutching the cheque he had thrust into her hands, so it must have happened.

She wrenched her eyes away from the door and her legs feeling suddenly weak, she sat down and blinked at the cheque in her hand made out to Jemma Nokes, and for the five thousand pounds she had asked for. She then did what she had intended doing all along and tore it up into tiny pieces. She felt some satisfaction in that act, but for the rest of the day until the time she went to bed, her previous intention of trying to come to some conclusion of what she would tell Oliver, was barely given a thought.

In bed her mind went over and over again every word Karn Fellingham had said to her believing she was Crystabella Nokes. It was clear he didn't believe her sister in love with Mark, and she felt again the same fury she had felt with him when he had more or less said that Christine's only interest in a man was the size of his bank balance. He couldn't be more wrong; Christine wasn't like that. When she had lived at home, although it was true all her escorts had been rather well to do, it had been simply because she could have her pick of anybody; the size of their bank account had been unimportant.

Jemma tried to recall if her sister had ever gone out with anyone who hadn't pulled up at their door in at least a Jag, but couldn't, then thrust the thought away from her as being disloyal. Christine probably had gone out with the more impecunious of the male species, only she couldn't remember.

She turned her thoughts back to Karn Fellingham. He had had a rough aggression about him, and since he could write out a cheque for five thousand without turning a hair he must obviously not be short of a penny or two. He looked shrewd too, and it amazed her that since he had never met Christine, but knowing she was going around with Mark, knowing where she lived, he must also know that she was a photographic model, how with all the shrewdness she had seen in his face, had he ever thought she, with her unmade-up face, could be a photographic model?

Jemma nipped out of bed and switched on the centre light, then went to stare at her face in the dressing table mirror. She saw nothing there that would inspire any camera man to go into raptures. Straight brown hair—true, it did have the red lights in it Christine had spoken of that day, but nothing in her view very spectacular about it. Her green eyes, she thought, were her best feature. Her nose wasn't bad as noses went, being straight and delicate-looking, but in her view her mouth was just a shade too full to ever be called beautiful. Her study of her face ended abruptly as she heard sounds indicating that Mark had brought Christine home. She hoped Mark wouldn't be staying too long, and much as she would rather not have to upset Christine—she had enough to worry about as it was while she was so anxious about the possibility of losing her flat—she would have to tell her about Karn Felling-ham's visit.

It seemed an age before she heard the outer door close, though it was only about twenty minutes later. Then, sure Mark had gone and knowing with Christine dashing off to Greece first thing in the morning there would be no time to talk to her then, Jemma pulled on her robe and went into the living room.

Christine stood in the centre of the room looking more or less as faultless as she had done when she had gone out. But she was completely unaware that Jemma had joined her, engrossed as she was in studying what she was hold-ing in her hands. Jemma went further into the room and Christine looked up.

'Not asleep yet? I thought you were the type who was

always in bed by ten o'clock.'

If it was her intention to imply that she thought her sister only one step up from a country bumpkin, Jemma had more important things on her mind than to notice.

'What have you got there?' she asked, her attention caught by the flash of gold Christine was holding.

'Do you like it?' she asked, offering out a gold bracelet for inspection. 'Mark bought it for me this afternoon.'

'It's lovely,' said Jemma, taking the bracelet that seemed to be made of solid gold from her. She wanted to ask if accepting Mark's valuable gift, the price of which she couldn't begin to guess at, meant she and Mark were about to be engaged. But Christine was taking the bracelet from her and saying:

'Well, I'm for bed.'

'You had a visitor not long after you had gone out,' Jemma said quickly, before her sister had taken many steps towards the door of her room.

Christine stopped and half turned. 'Oh, who?' she asked carelessly.

'Karn Fellingham.'

'Mark's uncle?' Jemma had her full attention now. 'What did he want?'

'He-he ...' Knowing she was about to hurt her, Jemma had difficulty in bringing the words out. 'He wanted to—to buy you off,' she said softly, all her sympathy for her in her voice as she waited for Christine to either be furious, the way she had been, or to burst into tears that Karn Fellingham should try and spoil something that was beautiful between her and Mark.

To her astonishment, Christine burst out laughing. 'He didn't?' she said. 'Oh, marvellous! Did he give you any idea of how much he thought it was worth?'

'I ... He ... Aren't you upset? I thought ...' she broke off as Christine didn't look to be at all upset. In a bewildered voice Jemma told her, 'He asked me if I was you,' and went on to tell her why at first she had let him believe she was, but how in the end she had been too furious to disabuse him of the idea.

Christine received this piece of information with none of her good humour disappearing. Perhaps she didn't realise what she was telling her, Jemma thought, her bewilderment growing that Christine thought the whole matter was something to giggle at. Though she couldn't think how she could tell her more plainly.

'So,' Christine queried, 'what happened when he'd established that you were Crystabella Nokes?'

'He told me to keep away from Mark, to let him concentrate on his studies, then asked how much I would take to cut him out of my life.'

That Christine was now taking in every word was evident by the fact that she gave up all intention of going to bed and went and sat down on the settee.

'And I suppose at that point you lost that temper of yours and told him to get out,' she said, no longer smiling.

Jemma hadn't realised she had that much of a temper that Christine should remember it and remark upon it, she had thought her temper had been left behind with her teens. But that was getting away from the point.

'I was angry, yes,' she admitted. 'But I haven't lost my temper in years.' She was amazed now to recall how icily cold she had felt in her anger with Karn Fellingham. 'He asked me how much, and I called his bluff by asking for five thousand.'

She rather thought Christine would now show the fury that had been absent after she had confessed she had asked for five thousand pounds under the pretence of being her, but her sister was smiling again, apparently thinking it was a huge joke.

'And what did he say to that?' she wanted to know.

'He didn't bat an eyelid,' Jemma told her, beginning to feel impatient that Christine wasn't reacting at all in the way she had thought she would, in a way anyone would with an ounce of common decency in them. 'He just took out his cheque book and wrote out a cheque for five thousand pounds.'

That took the smile off her face, momentarily at any rate. 'He didn't!' she gasped, then went on to ask, 'Where did you put it? Let me see it.'

'I ripped it up as soon as he had gone,' said Jemma, not liking at all the greedy light that had come into her sister's eyes.

'Oh, Jemma, you take the biscuit,' she groaned. 'Whatever did you do that for?'

It was Jemma's turn to gasp. 'You wouldn't have cashed it?' she said, astounded, forgetting for the moment the cheque had been made out in her name. 'You wouldn't have let the bribe of money split you and Mark, would you?'

'Of course not,' Christine came back promptly, but there was a hard look in her eyes that Jemma had never seen there before, and she hated that she couldn't wholly believe she was telling her the truth. 'What do you take me for?' she added, and sent Jemma such a warm smile that Jemma immediately wondered how she could think Christine had changed in any way from the lovable elder sister she had always been.

They talked for a few minutes more on the subject of Karn Fellingham, Christine telling her not to give him another thought, since it was most unlikely he would call at the flat again since he was now of the opinion his duty to Mark was done, and asking what he had looked like. Jemma had no trouble in describing the cold arrogance of the man, but when her sister asked after his age, she wasn't sure.

'Late thirties, I would think. He had a touch of grey in his hair, though that could be hereditary rather than denote his age,' she said, then she thought to ask if he was an estate agent.

'Estate agent?' Christine echoed. 'Good lord, no. He does "something in the City". He's the head of an organisation that dabbles in stocks and shares, I think. A foot-loose bachelor as rich as they come, by all accounts. Whatever made you think he was an estate agent?'

'Mark said something about seeing if his uncle had anything going when you were telling him how worried you were about the possibility of having to find somewhere else to live, so I thought . . .'

'Oh, that,' said Christine, and looked worried again at the prospect of having to leave her flat. Then getting to her feet and once more moving towards her bedroom door, 'He was left a lot of property by his grandfather. Mark had the idea of asking him if he has a flat coming vacant in the near future.' She bit her lip anxiously, then said wearily, 'But from what you've just told me, I can see once Karn Fellingham knows that any flat Mark enquires about is intended for me, I shan't stand a cat in hell's chance of getting it.'

CHAPTER TWO

JEMMA was up early the next morning to see her sister off. It amazed her that after a very few hours' sleep Christine appeared bandbox-fresh, and she couldn't refrain from commenting on it.

'Make-up, Jemma; hides a multitude of sins. Must dash. Treat the flat as if it were your own, but keep your hands off any of my boy-friends!'

Jemma had to grin when Christine had hurriedly departed, sure her sister had been joking and doubting she had a boy-friend who was so near-sighted he would prefer her when Christine would be back shortly.

She sobered as the thought came that Christine no longer had a string of boy-friends, and she was once more certain that her sister was in love with Mark. That being the case she would have dropped all her other escorts. Mark's name was the only name she had heard her mention at any rate, and she was sure that secure in Mark's love her sister could laugh at any threat Karn Fellingham could put in the way of their happiness. She wondered if they would wait until Mark had finished his studies before they married, and remembering the bracelet Christine had shown her last night, thought he must have plenty of money, so reasoned that was it, that they must be waiting before they announced their plans.

Jemma thought of Christine married to Mark, and a gentle expression crossed her face. From what she had seen of him, she thought he would make a lovely brother-in-law. Her gentle expression faded, as thoughts of marriage reminded her she had done nothing about coming up with the answer she had to give Oliver. Really she should get down to thinking about him. What was she going to do? Did she want to marry him?

The day before Christine was due to come home sped quickly on. Seldom bored, Jemma explored London each day and came home at night footsore and happy to go to bed with a book. She had taken to London like a duck to water, and was loving every moment of her holiday, the thought having crossed her mind more than once that she wouldn't mind living here.

But on the day Christine was due home, since she had no idea what time she would arrive, she decided to stay at home and give the flat a clean through. Dressed in her faded jeans with a loose shirt, she was guiding the vacuum cleaner over the sitting room carpet when a banging on the door made her aware that someone had probably been ringing for an age only she hadn't heard them, before resorting to try and bang the door down. Switching off the vacuum cleaner, she glanced at her watch. Ten o'clock was a bit early for callers, and with the living room looking all anyhow with all the furniture pushed to one side she hoped it wasn't anyone expecting to come in.

Pushing back the strand of hair that had escaped from the rubber band at the back of her hair, Jemma went to open the door as another thud sounded on its panels, and had to quickly stifle the impulse to slam the door to again as she recognised Karn Fellingham standing there, looking none the sweeter than the last time she had seen him.

He took his time studying her, his eyes travelling, insultingly she thought, from the top of her brown head over her firm bustline, down to her hips and to the ends of her moccasin-clad feet, before his cold eyes returned to her face, his glance lingering over her mouth before he looked long and hard into her eyes.

Although his silent scrutiny riled her, she was glad his

silence gave her the chance to get in first.

'To what do I owe this unexpected *pleasure*?' she asked
with more coolness than she felt, congratulating herself that
she had been able to bring out the word 'pleasure' with
just about the same amount of emphasis as he had the time
he had used it.

'Do you want a free for all on your doorstep?' he asked
aggressively, letting her know he had recognised she was
ready to do battle with him, and his expression telling her
that in his opinion she had lost the fight before it got
started.

'*Do* come in,' she said sweetly, coming away from the
door so that he could follow her. 'Though I'm afraid I can't
ask you to sit down, I'm in the middle of cleaning.' She
ignored his look that told her he was surprised a girl of her
type ever pushed a vacuum cleaner around. 'But perhaps I
can hope that this visit will be as brief as your previous
one.'

He ignored her sarcasm. 'You're a cheat, Miss Nokes,'
he made no bones about telling her. 'There are a lot of
other names I could call you too, if just the sight of you
and all you stand for didn't sicken me to my stomach.'

Too late she realised just why he had called. He must
have found out she wasn't Crystabella, she saw, her
thoughts going off at a tangent, her own stomach not feeling so very strong either now. He had seen Mark? Seen a
picture of Christine? Mark had told him Crystabella had
her sister staying with her? However he had found out it
was clear from the look of loathing that was coming her
way that he knew she had duped him. Clear he thought she
had paid that cheque he had given her into her account
and had now come to sort her out. And what had been his
parting remark the last time she had seen him? 'Try
double-crossing me and you'll live to regret it.' Oh God,
and albeit sarcastically, she had invited him in! It took a

lot of courage to look him in the eyes, but she managed it as she told him with a lofty air she thought remarkable:

'Your opinion of me, I assure you, will in no way interfere with my night's sleep. Nor will the fact that you appear to have a delicate stomach.' She saw his eyes narrow that she was not to be cowed by any harsh name he could think of for her, and decided right then that she wasn't going to be cowed. If she had paid his cheque into her account instead of tearing it up, then in her considered opinion it was only what he deserved for the way he had tried to part Christine and Mark. 'Why exactly in your highly esteemed view am I a cheat?' she challenged, her lofty air slipping as she saw his hands clench into fists at his sides, causing her to wonder if he was measuring the distance to her jaw.

'You haven't even that much honesty in you to admit you quite well know without my having to tell you, have you?' he said, disgust obvious in his face without the need of the snarl in his voice. Jemma knew he hadn't finished yet, not by a long chalk. 'Barely an hour after I gave you a cheque which was the agreed figure for you keeping your designing talons off Mark, you were sweet-talking him into buying you an item of jewellery he could in no way afford.'

'The bracelet,' said Jemma before she could stop herself, as the remembrance of the bracelet Mark had bought for Christine came to her. And then, startlingly, following that remembrance came the realisation that he didn't know, Karn Fellingham *still* didn't know that she wasn't Crystabella.

'The bracelet,' he agreed, and she saw that in his view that with her knowledge of the existence of the bracelet she had just confirmed everything he had accused her of. 'It's unfortunate for you that the jeweller's assistant recognised you from your magazine pictures and recalled the sale without any difficulty. It was near closing time, she told me, she was anxious to get away, but she had to stay because Miss Nokes couldn't make up her mind which gold bracelet she wanted before she eventually settled for the most expensive one. You were much too eager to grab everything you could,' he told her stonily, 'and because of your greed I consider the contract I made with you null and void. If you have any thoughts of going on a spending spree with my money, I advise you to forget it—I've cancelled the cheque I gave you.'

'Cancelled it?' Jemma echoed, not meaning to say that at all, but feeling too surprised at the detective work he had done to think straight.

'You delayed too long in paying the money into your account,' he told her. 'That cheque is not worth the paper it's written on.'

'I ripped it up,' she said, glad to have the anger that was roaring to life in her under control.

'Like hell you did,' he snapped, making it clear he wasn't going to believe anything she said. 'And of course you have the torn up fragments all ready to show me.'

'I threw them away . . .'

'Of course you did,' he sneered. 'Well, that cheque is worthless to you now, Jemma Nokes, and if your delay in presenting it to your bank was because you thought there might be richer pickings by hanging on to Mark, permit me to tell you you've backed the wrong horse. Mark may appear to have unlimited funds; I've no doubt he's wined and dined you royally, but unlike your last boy-friend, Rodney Haden—a pity his wife called him back to heel, wasn't it?—while Mark might appear to be in the same financial bracket as the Hadens, let me inform you that the only money Mark Stevens has is the allowance I make him. An allowance he has already overspent,' Karn Fellingham was fairly biting into her now. 'The bank have been in touch with me; Mark didn't have any money in his account to clear the cheque for that little five-hundred item. So you see, your favours to him are being paid for from money he will no doubt get around to asking me to advance him.'

Jemma made an instinctive movement with her right hand that he could insult her so, have no qualms about stating that Christine slept with Mark for what she could get out of him. Fury at his insult ousted the cool front she was showing him.

But the blow she would have struck him never landed, for he seized her wrist in a brutal hold. 'I can hit harder than you,' he told her tersely, leaving her in no doubt that had she hit him then she would have been knocked senseless by that fist she had been wary of connecting with her jaw. He waited until he saw from her eyes that she had changed her mind about hitting him, and threw her wrist from his hold with such force that she knew he felt tainted by having touched her.

'So now, you cheating bitch, now that you know Mark is never likely to be able to keep you in the style to which you would like to become accustomed, perhaps now you'll leave him alone!'

Jemma still wasn't very convinced that he wouldn't set about her, but for Christine's sake, for the sake of the love she was sure her sister had for Mark, she just couldn't let this man walk in here and think he could say what he liked.

'It's never occurred to you that I might be in love with Mark, that I might want to marry him regardless of whether he has any money or not?' she asked, taking a step away from him to get out of range should he decide that actions spoke louder than words.

'Just who are you trying to kid?' he asked her nastily. 'The only person you love, Miss Nokes, is yourself. You were quite happy being Rodney Haden's mistress until you found out Thelma Haden held the purse strings, then as soon as she found out about your affair and cut off the money supply, you dropped him before he knew what was happening.'

Thelma and Rodney Haden were names Jemma had never heard of before, and what he was saying about her sister sickened her. But since, not knowing any of the facts—and she wasn't prepared to listen to any of his biased thinking anyway; Christine wasn't like that, she knew she wasn't—Jemma could only argue on a matter she did know something about.

'All that is beside the point, surely,' she said, and saw a look of disgust cross his face that she could so easily dismiss what he thought had been her part in trying to break up a marriage. 'You can keep your money, Mr Fellingham, I wouldn't touch a penny of it. And as for leaving Mark alone, I can assure you that if and when he asks me to marry him, I shall be only too pleased to accept.'

She saw his hands clench again, but stood her ground. If his only method of browbeating her was to physically assault her, and one blow from him would be enough to flatten her, then she wasn't going to stand there and let him do it.

'And if you have any idea of using bullying tactics to try and get me to back down then you can think again. I don't know much about you, Mr Karn Fellingham, but I shouldn't think you'd like to see your name plastered across the national dailies when I summon you for assault.'

'Summon me for assault!' he echoed, just as though the idea of giving her a hiding had never entered his head. 'Allow me to inform you, Miss Nokes, that I wouldn't soil my hands in touching you.' He paused, his eyes watchful, then a considering look came over his face. 'Though on second thoughts—why the hell not?'

He took that pace or two that brought him close up to her, and Jemma, her anger getting out of control at all the vile slurs he had heaped on Christine through her, was growing too incensed to be frightened of him any more, and stayed exactly where she was.

'I doubt Mark has sufficient experience yet to make the grade as a first-rate lover—though no doubt you've been able to teach him a thing or two—but since we're talking of punishment—try this for size.'

And before she could duck out of the way, her fear returning jet-propelled as he made a grab for her, Karn Fellingham had hauled her into his arms and she wasn't being knocked senseless. Not by blows at any rate, for he was kissing her, and she had never been kissed like it before.

His first kiss was an insult as his mouth forced her lips apart and he made no pretence of being gentle. She felt his hard muscular body up against hers and fought him with everything that was in her as she felt his hands tearing at the buttons on her shirt, intent, it seemed, on proving that the sort of woman he thought she was didn't deserve any better treatment.

Alarm mingled with anger when she felt his hands bitingly cruel on her naked rib cage. She felt those same hands move to her hips where he pulled her even closer against him so that not so much as a postage stamp could have got between their two bodies. And then as she wrestled with him, her alarm growing at what the outcome might be, she tried to get her hands up to his face to rake her nails through his skin—for if he was all set to rape her, then she wasn't going to be the only one to be nursing wounds—the hard pressure of his insulting kiss eased, became persuasive, inviting, was a totally different sort of kiss. And suddenly, incomprehensibly, with no rhyme or reason to it, as her hands came into contact with the sides of his face, all the urge to score her nails on his flesh vanished.

Something was happening inside her that was outside her experience and the fight went out of her. She knew she should be hitting out at him, but she couldn't as her hands moved from his face to drop down to his shoulders, and all she could do then was hang on. Because, senselessly, insanely, while she hated him and all those vile things he had said about Christine, he was making her body come alive in a way Oliver had never been able to.

The battle she was fighting now was not with him, but within herself. She must not respond, was the only clear thought that presented itself as Karn Fellingham's expert fingers made a nonsense of her thought waves as he made music on her spinal column, his mouth seeking at her throat. She clutched on to him, knowing she should be pushing him away rather than hanging on. Then his mouth claimed hers once more and her head was swimming so she had no clear recollection of where she was, of what she was doing, and this time he had no need to force her lips apart.

She still had no clear idea where she was, when suddenly she became aware that she was standing unsupported. Those hard arms were no longer moulding her to him. Jemma opened her eyes, and almost rocked where she stood. For Karn Fellingham, it appeared, had tired of whatever experiment he had been conducting and was standing all of a yard away from her with only the merest tinge of darkened colour under his skin to give any indication that he had had any part in making her senses sing.

Bitterly ashamed of herself, her colour seared, only to fade and leave her cheeks pale, as it came to her that not only did he have no intention of raping her—and that word was long since obsolete—but that he had hauled her into his arms at first perhaps only to insult her, but then as an experiment to see just how far she would go. Oh God, she thought, she'd have to tell him she wasn't Christine now. She just couldn't let him go away thinking her professed feelings for Mark went for nothing the instant another man took her in his arms.

'Karn ...' she began, bit her lip that that wasn't right either, and knew she wasn't anywhere near ready yet to think clearly. 'Mr Fellingham ...' she began again.

'Save it,' he said, looking at her with that look from down his nose she loathed. Then he defeated her completely by saying, 'Had I been in any doubt that you were sincere about Mark, then I've just had my answer, haven't I?' His lip actually curled in a sneer when next he spoke, and Jemma hated him at that moment more than she had thought it possible to hate anyone. 'You're no more in love with Mark than you are with anyone but yourself,' he almost spat at her. 'You'd come on for anyone with the right bank balance!'

Pride stormed in as he made for the door, and it was as much for herself as for Christine that she said, 'Not at all, Mr Fellingham. Since you've elected to be my—enemy, then surely you appreciate I had to find out just how far *you* would go.'

It was weak, pathetic even, and she could tell Karn Fellingham was not deceived. He didn't even bother to reply, but gave her one long contemptuous look, said threateningly, 'Leave Mark alone,' and went.

By the time Christine arrived home in the late afternoon, Jemma had come a long way to recovering from the assault Karn Fellingham had made on her senses. Too often during the day she had relived that scene with him, and was nowhere nearer to analysing what had come over her. But while waiting for Christine, after long hours spent in thought, with no answer to what it was in her chemistry that had made her act that way—and with him of all people—she had come to one very solid conclusion. She had no need any longer to delve into the 'should she, should she nots' of marrying Oliver. One thing that shouted above all others was that never in a million years would Oliver make her senses sing the way Karn Fellingham had done, and what was more, she didn't want him to try.

Having come to that conclusion, or rather, having that conclusion shouted at her, all that remained was for her to tell Oliver that she wasn't going to marry him. She wasn't going to enjoy doing that, she knew, but she knew also that should he try to get her to change her mind then he would be wasting his time.

Quite when or why she began to think it might be a good idea to leave Elvington and come to London to live, to make a career for herself, she wasn't sure, though she suspected the thought had come because she didn't want to think about the task that faced her in telling Oliver of her decision, that mixed with a determination that she had wasted enough time in thinking about Karn Fellingham and what he could do to her well brought up impulses, plus the fact that each time she thought of Karn Fellingham it made her furious the way he was trying to split up Christine and Mark.

Already she was half way to being in love with London, loving its bustle, its life. Elvington, dear little place though it was, was really a very sleepy little town. She admitted now that she had been restless lately, and couldn't help wondering if it had taken the—yes, it had to be said—the excitement of Karn Fellingham's kisses to wake her up, to shake her normal thinking into realising that if she was going to do anything with her life, then it was up to her alone to get on and do it. Karn Fellingham had shown her she wasn't ready for marriage yet—how could she be when she had kissed back so indiscriminately? She was too used to the place she had been born in, had grown up in, lovely though it was, and was experiencing an overwhelming urge to try her wings. She would never be more than a shorthand-typist-cum-dogsbody in Elvington. But if she came to London who knew ... Excitement grew in her as she weighed up all the pros and cons, knowing in her heart that her decision was already made.

She bottled down her excitement when Christine walked in, seeing her sister looked tired though she still managed to look elegant in her tiredness as she dropped her suitcase down on the floor and sank down on to the settee.

'Lord, I'm whacked!' she stated. 'If anyone ever tells you being a photographic model is easy, refer them to me.'

'I'll get you a cup of tea,' said Jemma, leaving her to go into the kitchen.

Christine had figured many times in her thoughts too since Karn Fellingham had left. Uppermost in her mind was the feeling of guilt that she had responded to him the way she had with him believing she was Crystabella Nokes. She would have to confess to Christine about that, of course, everything in her told her she must, though she squirmed at having to do so. She had thought also of the vile things Karn Fellingham had said about her sister, and hated him with a greater intensity that he should put the doubt in her mind for even a second, the doubt that had asked how well had she known Christine anyway since Christine had rarely spent an evening in when she had lived in Elvington? She tossed the doubt aside. She wasn't going to turn against her sister, she just wasn't. The Christine she remembered had always been ambitious, but that was natural, and with her looks she could have anybody she wanted. And, Jemma thought, since it was Mark she wanted, then if she had anything to do with it, Mark she should have. The kettle boiled, the tea made, Jemma took the tray into the living room where Christine had kicked off her shoes and was lying back on the settee. Somehow or other she was going to have to tell her about Karn Fellingham's visit, but not just yet; she'd wait until Christine had had a cup of tea first.

'Just what the doctor ordered,' Christine declared, stretching out one perfectly manicured hand for the cup and saucer Jemma was offering. 'Any post?'

'I'll get it,' said Jemma, getting up and fetching what the postman had delivered for her sister in her absence.

'Uh-uh,' Christine grimaced, placing two letters of lesser importance to one side and staring at the white envelope she held in her left hand.

'Something wrong?' Jemma asked, wondering why she didn't open the envelope and get it over with seeing that she had recognised the writing on the envelope and didn't look very happy about it.

'You could say that. My dear landlord has never written yet to tell me any good news.' Christine ripped open the envelope, then scanned the contents. 'Bless his stingy old heart,' she said humourlessly. 'He says that under no circumstances will he allow me to stay on when my lease expires. Underlines, no less, that he cannot consider renewing my lease and that he'll be glad if I'll look for alternative accommodation straight away, *and* that should I stay one day longer than the said date, he'll seek the courts' help in evicting me.'

'Oh, Chris,' Jemma said softly, all her sympathy with her in her plight. 'What will you do?'

'If I knew, duckie, I'd tell you.' Christine put the letter back in its envelope, swallowed the remains of her tea and said, 'Give me a refill, there's a dear, I'll go and telephone Mark.'

Jemma poured her another cup of tea while Christine went into her bedroom to make her call. She wasn't offended that she wanted to make her call in private. If she was in love she wouldn't want anyone, no matter how close, hearing the things she wanted to say to her beloved after a five days' absence either. That thought endorsed for her that her decision not to marry Oliver had been the right one. She had been away from Oliver nine days now, and apart from needing privacy to tell him she wasn't going to marry him, there wasn't a thing she wanted to say to him that the whole world couldn't hear.

When Christine came back from making her phone call, she still had a faintly worried look about her, which caused Jemma to delay telling her about Karn Fellingham's visit. She had decided against mentioning that Mark didn't have any money; she saw no point in doing so since Christine was so in love with him it wouldn't matter to her anyway, and didn't see it as her role to poke her nose into something that had nothing to do with her.

'What have you been doing with yourself?' Christine asked, reaching for her cup and saucer.

'Behaving like a tourist,' Jemma told her, 'and loving every minute of it.' And then, excitement growing in her voice, she mentioned some of the other thoughts she had had that day. 'Actually, I thought I might leave Elvington and look for a job in London.'

'You really have loved every minute of it haven't you,' said Christine. 'Though I never could understand why you stayed in the backwoods so long, but thought you must have something going with this Oliver bod Mother wrote and said you were dating. You're not serious about him?'

'No, I'm not serious about him,' Jemma admitted quietly.

'Well, that's a blessing anyway. If you bothered with yourself a bit more you could do far better for yourself than a bank clerk.'

Jemma's eyes widened incredulously at this. It was so out of character, she thought, for Christine to talk so derisively of Oliver's job. He was in a respected profession, and had she loved him it wouldn't have mattered to her what job he did.

'Don't look so put out, love. One has to be a realist in this world. There's always someone ready to do you one in the eye if you don't get in first.'

Jemma remained silent, and could only think that this new way of thinking from Christine had only come about since she had entered the modelling world with its fierce competition.

'You'll find looking for a flat here won't be easy,' her sister told her. 'You'll probably have to make do with a bedsit for a while unless you can get to share with some-body. I'd have you here to stay with me, but I don't think it would work; I need to be alone sometimes.'

Jemma hadn't quite got round to thinking of where she was going to live, and appreciated that Christine must want solitude from time to time after the exacting work she did, though she refrained from mentioning that she would be flat-hunting herself before the end of next month was out if she didn't want to be taken to court.

Christine soon came round from the weariness of her journey, and as she began to tell Jemma some of the details of her work over the last five days, the opportunity didn't present itself for Jemma to tell her of Karn Fellingham's visit.

It was with a guilty conscience that Jemma went to bed that night. True, she hadn't had much chance to say any-thing on the subject of Karn Fellingham since Mark had wasted no time in calling at the flat once he knew Christine was home, and she couldn't very well tell her anything while his nephew was present; she shied from even her sister knowing of the wantonness of her behaviour, so how could she tell her with Mark there? Besides which, she appeased her conscience, how could she hurt Christine by letting her know how thoroughly Karn Fellingham de-spised her? And anyway, he would soon know he had kissed the wrong girl when he met the real Crystabella Nokes, as he would, for Mark was sure to introduce them before long.

Jemma spent the days remaining of her holiday in scouring London for somewhere to live. Her mind was by now firmly made up to give up her job and move to London. Though what her parents were going to say, she didn't know; and she still had to tell Oliver of her decision.

As Christine had prophesied, the task she had set herself in looking for a flat was not an easy one. And after traipsing round what she thought must be the whole length and breadth of London for three days, she had still not found anywhere.

Doggedly she refused to give in, and on the fourth day she had her reward, for she was lucky in finding a very small flat that comprised one bedroom and a sitting room, with the smallest kitchen she had ever seen, and a shared bathroom. She thought she had been able to keep her face expressionless when the size of the rent required was mentioned, and agreed to take it while her brain was doing the calculation on her finances and reasoning that salaries would be higher in London than they were where she came from.

As flats went it was a particularly depressing one, but she was in no mind to let that put her off. If she let this one go heaven alone knew when she would come across another one that suited her pocket as well as her eyes.

'Shall I pay you the rent now?' she asked the chesty Mrs Parkin, who had wheezed up to the first floor to show her the rooms. She wasn't taking any chances on the flat being taken by someone else the moment her back was turned.

'If you don't mind, miss,' Mrs Parkin said, lighting up a cigarette and having a prolonged coughing session that made Jemma want to dash for a glass of water or something to help her. Mrs Parkin wiped her eyes, her coughing done with, without commenting on it, her cough apparently being as much a part of her as breathing.

Jemma couldn't wait to get back to tell Christine. Her thoughts spiralled upwards. Having thought to take her cheque book with her she had paid Mrs Parkin two months' rent, not being sure when she would be able to get up to London again. She would have to work out a month's notice from her present job. There would be her clothes and books, trinkets and lord knew what else to pack. There would be saucepans to buy and ... Her thoughts took flight as she became excited by her decision to be a new Jemma Nokes. She had already decided she would fare better if she was on the spot when making job applications, and she had some savings which she hoped were going to last her until she had found what she was looking for. Her eyes shone as she thought how she was going to be the best secretary there ever was—or near to it anyway.

Christine wasn't in when she reached the flat, but none of her enthusiasm had waned when she eventually came home.

'Jammy,' was Christine's comment when she told her her good news.

'Well, it isn't such a great flat,' she replied, thinking perhaps she might well have overstated her description of it in her enthusiasm. 'In actual fact you'd probably think it's a little bit grotty, but,' enthusiasm was on her again, 'I intend to colour-wash all the walls; they're a sort of army surplus khaki at the moment.'

Her sister really was as nice as she had always thought she was, Jemma thought, a surge of love for her coming over her when the two girls went to their rooms that night. Christine needn't have offered to let her come here for the few days it would take for her to splash some white paint about her new abode. But she had. She had said quite naturally and without any trace of the cold, calculating bitch Karn Fellingham thought she was, 'Mother and

Father would have a fit if they thought you were moving into a slum, you'd better stay here till the paint's dry.'

So, Jemma thought, and actually thumbed her nose at the man who had started off her new thinking, you are one hundred per cent wrong in your assessment of my sister, Mr overbearing, over—over-everything Fellingham!

CHAPTER THREE

To put it mildly, her parents were rather shaken when Jemma told them her plans for the future. The news of everything Christine was doing had come first, and then as the three of them sat round the table having dinner, her father asked and how had she got on in the great metropolis, she knew she had to tell them now or she would never have the nerve to tell them at all.

'Actually, Dad, I liked it very much. In—er—actual fact —er——' she looked at her mother, sensed that she knew she was stammering to get out something that would affect the three of them, took a deep breath and said, 'Mum, Dad, I've ... I've decided I want to live and work in London.'

She couldn't bear to look at them as she said it, couldn't bear it if they were hurt. She felt awful in the shocked silence that followed. These two people had fed, clothed, brought her up, had guided her in the various stages of her development, and for all they had never said so in words, she knew herself loved by them. That love was there in everything they had done for her. And she felt wretched and ungrateful that she wanted to set about discovering a fresh new world away from them. Then her father, the first to recover, was saying gently:

'Well, we never expected to have you with us for ever, did we, Mother?'

And her mother was answering slowly, 'No—no, we didn't. But Jemma isn't like Christine. Christine can take care of herself, but ...' her voice tailed off, and Jemma just had to look at her mother then. Of the two, she had expected her father to be the more upset, but at the shimmer of tears in her mother's eyes she was out of her chair and going to put her arms around her.

'I won't go,' she said, her impulsive nature getting the better of her fine plans, unable to bear seeing her mother battling against tears.

'Yes, you will,' Ellen Nokes came back. 'You're a softie, Jemma, always have been. But if this going to live in London is what you want, then go to London you will. All we ask is that you keep in touch with us, remember you have a home here.'

Jemma saw a look pass between her parents. It was as if they were saying that an equally loved Christine had gone to London too, but apart from the very occasional flying visit she had forgotten she had any parents.

'I'll write to you every week,' she promised, 'and you'll probably get fed up with me turning up on your doorstep!'

They were late going to bed that night, Jemma telling them about her flat and how she was going to stay with Christine for a few nights while she was getting it in order.

'What's the furniture like?' her mother wanted to know.

'Not too bad,' Jemma told her, having every intention of getting in there with a load of elbow grease. 'There are a couple of chunky chairs like the two belonging to this suite, they could do with new covers, but ...'

'You can have the old ones from the suite,' said Ellen Nokes, who lived up to her husband's teasing of never throwing anything away. 'They're not in bad condition, we'll go up into the attic tomorrow and look at them and see if there's anything else you can use while we're up there.'

On Sunday morning, Jemma thought she had better telephone Oliver before she went to the attic with her mother. She was dreading seeing him, but knew what she had to tell him couldn't be said over the phone, and since it wasn't fair to keep him waiting for her answer any longer, she went and dialled his number.

'Thank you for the card,' he said, and if that was a polite reference to the fact that he would have appreciated a letter far more than the picture postcard she had sent him, then perhaps he had a point there.

'C-can I see you today, Oliver?' she asked, not sounding very happy in her request.

'We'll go somewhere tonight,' he stated.

No, she didn't want that, didn't want a date with him. 'I—I just wanted to talk to you for a few minutes, that's all.'

'That sounds ominous,' he commented.

Without telling him everything there was to tell him now, and she owed it to him, she thought, to tell him face to face, though she was sorely tempted to funk it, there wasn't a thing she could answer to that.

'I'll come over now,' he said decisively.

'Y-yes, all right.'

Jemma put the phone down and saw her mother coming along the hall, who on seeing she had finished her call, asked, 'Ready?'

'Oliver's coming over.'

Ellen Nokes studied her daughter's unsmiling face. 'He's serious about you, isn't he?' she asked. Jemma bit her lip and nodded. Her mother had no need to ask if she was serious about him, she wouldn't be going to live in London if she was. 'He's not the reason you're leaving home, is he?'

Jemma didn't need to think about it. 'No,' she said honestly. Oliver might have something to do with the realisation that she was in a rut, and that horrible Karn Fellingham's kisses had shown her that Oliver was not for her, but she wasn't leaving just to get away from Oliver.

'Good,' said Mrs Nokes, then practically, 'We'll go up to the attic this afternoon.'

Tactfully her mother was in the kitchen when Oliver arrived, and when Jemma took him into the sitting room and noted absently that the Sunday papers weren't in their usual spot, she realised her mother was far more understanding than she had thought and had most likely got her father in the kitchen reading his Sunday paper whether he liked it or not.

Jemma turned to Oliver as soon as he had closed the door behind them. 'Thank you for coming over, Oliver,' she said, and not sure how to continue but wishing it all said, 'I've had time to think about—about what you asked me.' She saw she had his full attention, saw he looked almost eager, so she added quickly, 'But I'm very sorry, Oliver, I can't marry you.'

'Can't marry me? You mean ...'

'I mean I—I appreciate you asking me, but I ...'

'You need more time to get used to the idea?'

'No—No. It isn't that.' She had already had two weeks, if she thought about it for another two years her answer would still be the same. 'We've been good friends, and I've always enjoyed being out with you. We've had some good times, but ...'

'We could have good times again,' he interrupted her, his thin features looking resolved. 'I won't take no for an answer, Jemma. You laugh with me, you feel comfortable with me. Hell, the very way you've been with me has given me every indication that you care for me.'

She saw then that he wasn't going to take her refusal without argument and wished then that she had taken the easy way out and told him over the telephone.

'It's no good, Oliver—I just don't love you.'

For a moment that seemed to stop him in his tracks, but he was made of sterner stuff than to let that put him off.

'I think you're too confused at the moment to know what you feel for me,' he told her. 'Just because I've allowed the way we've been together to go along at the pace you set you've been complacent in our relationship. I see now that I should have wooed you with a bit more passion, should have let you see that the kisses we have shared can be more thrilling than they have been—you wouldn't be wondering then whether you love me or not.'

Jemma had never heard Oliver talk like this before. Perhaps she *had* been complacent in there almost stagnant relationship. But one thing she did know was that she was certain she did not love him, and what was more, she was feeling uncomfortable that he could talk to her this way.

'Come here, Jemma,' he said, and when she refused to move, he came over to her and took her roughly in his arms.

'Please don't,' she begged, not afraid of what he would do but feeling more than anything sad that their friendship was going to end this way. 'It's no good, Oliver,' she added. Then what she had suspected was going to happen since his talk of passion missing from their relationship and from the tight way he was holding her became fact, and he was kissing her in a way he had never done before, the passion he had spoken of rearing its head.

If she had been worried about any latent promiscuity in her nature, the thought having sprung to life after she had responded so insanely to Karn Fellingham's kisses, then she needn't have worried at all. For there was no excitement for her when Oliver attempted to kiss her after the same fashion—though she had to own without Karn Fellingham's expertise—and all she felt was a greater sadness than ever.

'I'm sorry,' she mumbled when his arms had dropped slackly away, but her words were not really needed; her lack of response was more than sufficient to tell him he was wasting his time.

She cried when he had gone, thinking she had not handled that very well, and upset that she had hurt him for all she could not have answered his proposal any other way.

Her mother knew she had been crying when she joined them for lunch, her father too. But when he began to comment on it by saying, 'Hey, love, what ...' her mother headed him off by saying if he didn't start to carve the joint soon then everything else would be cold.

Jemma's notice at work was received with polite regret, though it was Mr Riley she worked specifically for and he would be off sick for another couple of months if he ever came back at all, following his massive stroke. But she hoped he would not be upset when she wasn't there if he did return, for she had always got on well with him.

She spent every spare moment in the month that followed in brushing up on her shorthand which had fallen into disuse, her sights firmly fixed on the career she would make for herself.

The attic had been teeming with all sorts of odds and ends she could make use of; pretty floral lampshades, two saucepans, dented and a bit battered, admittedly, but still useable, even a non-stick frying pan that had lost its non-stick.

'I shall need a furniture van to take all this stuff,' she said when she saw she wasn't going to cram it all into her luggage.

'Take what you can this time. It'll be a good excuse to rush back home and have your Noddy drinking mug topped up,' her father had tormented her.

But his teasing had deserted him when he stood with her mother at the station to see her off. 'You're a good girl, Jem,' he said, the shortened use of her name making her choke back tears. 'Look after yourself, baby.' And as she was getting into the train, having hugged her mother and told her she would be home for a weekend as soon as she was settled, her father pushed a folded cheque into her hands. 'Blow your savings on a splurge, and keep that for your nest egg,' he told her.

'But Dad, I don't want ...' she began to protest, only to have her mother interrupt.

'Take it, Jemma. We did the same for Christine. Living in London will be expensive and you'll most likely need it.'

She was glad to have a compartment to herself as the train chugged out of the station. She wouldn't cry, she told herself, but she did. The cheque her parents had given her was for five hundred pounds, and she wept some more when she saw the amount. They weren't badly off, but it must have made a dent in their savings.

She took her things straight to her new flat, winced slightly at the khaki walls, but turned her back on them, leaving her things packed as they were and went out straight away to have a reviving cup of tea in a nearby cafe, before searching the shops for brushes and paints. The sooner she got started, the sooner her new life would be under way.

It took her four days to get the flat looking like home. They were four back-breaking days, but when on Thursday afternoon she put down her paintbrush and stood back and admired her handiwork, she considered her efforts had been well worth while. She hesitated whether to return to Christine's that night. The smell of paint didn't seem so bad—or was it that she had got used to it? Then she remembered the dress Christine had asked her to sew the hem on that had come down, and not knowing if she wanted to wear it the next day, though she had plenty of others, she locked up her flat and made her way to her sister's.

'I'll be out from under your feet tomorrow,' Jemma told her when Christine came in after her date with Mark that evening. 'My flat is looking more like home now.'

'Lucky you,' said Christine, showing signs that she was more interested in her own imminent homelessness than in what Jemma had been able to do to make her flat comfortable. Jemma realised straight away that perhaps her remark had not been the most tactful in the circumstances as she witnessed the worried frown that came over her sister's features.

'Mark hasn't been able to do anything, I suppose?' she asked, and as Christine gave her an odd questioning look, she reminded her, 'He said he was going to ask his uncle if he had anything going, didn't he?'

'Fat chance,' was the sour reply. 'Oh, he asked him weeks ago, and Mark said he told him he was extremely sorry he couldn't help. But after the brush you had with him that time, I'll bet he had a hard job keeping his face straight while he said it.' She sighed, and muttered, 'The swine!' which caused Jemma to nod in full agreement. She could add a few more names to that!

Christine leant forward and extracted a cigarette from the cigarette box on the low table before her, lighting the long cylinder, inhaling deeply, then blowing the smoke out in one single stream. But this action seemed to do nothing to relieve her anxieties, which Jemma could see were getting on top of her, for she stood up and began a restless pacing about the room.

'I've more than half *expected* Mark to do something,' she said, as though thinking aloud. 'When I mentioned the flat to him tonight I thought ...' her voice tailed off as if suddenly she didn't want anyone else to know of her private thoughts, and she went and sat down again.

Jemma understood perfectly why she wanted to keep her thoughts private and her heart went out to her. Not only was Christine worried about the flat, but loving Mark as she did, she must be waiting for him to propose and finding the waiting getting her down. Why Mark hadn't proposed yet when she had seen for herself how very much in love with her he was, she couldn't fathom.

Her thoughts were rudely shattered by Christine suddenly exploding, 'God knows what I'm going to do,' as she again stood up, stubbed out her cigarette and went restlessly over to the window. 'I've asked everyone I can think of to look out for something for me, but friends have a nasty way of deserting you when you want something from them.'

Jemma could see she was getting worked up into quite a state, and it was so unusual for her to act this way, she wasn't sure of the best way to handle it. Christine usually had her emotions well under control, and that she was now showing herself to be a shade dramatic showed her clearly that it was coming home to her at last the plight she was in. She opted to keep quiet while her sister let off steam.

'Even that rat Rod Haden has decided to desert the sinking ship,' she said bitterly, and began her pacing again.

Rod Haden! Jemma had given little thought to what Karn Fellingham had said had gone on between her sister and Rodney Haden. She didn't believe a word he had told her, of course, and had no intention of saying anything to her about it; well, she couldn't very well, could she? Not since she hadn't been able to mention Karn Fellingham's last visit. But here was Christine freely describing Rodney Haden, and in embittered tones.

A disquiet started growing within her that had to be firmly squashed. No, she just wasn't going to believe her sister had been the mistress of a married man; it was disloyal to say the least. And she hated Karn Fellingham afresh that he could for an instant put such a doubt in her mind about her lovely sister.

'Rod Haden?' she queried, when Christine had stopped pacing up and down long enough for her to gain her attention. Perhaps if she could get her talking it would relax some of Christine's tensions; she seemed to be growing more strung up by the minute.

'Someone I used to know. Funny what short memories some people have,' she was told cynically. 'He once declared he'd do anything for me. Do you know,' she added rancidly, 'he's six feet tall, but scared stiff of that bitch of a wife of his.' She marched restlessly to the cigarette box and lit up another cigarette, missing entirely that Jemma had paled at what she had just said.

It couldn't be true, Jemma was thinking, her colour slowly returning as the shock of Christine's words left her. She was taking the wrong meaning of the words. Christine must have known him before he had married. Jemma couldn't bear to think that Karn Fellingham had been right in what he had said about her sister, and so she deliberately blocked her mind from further speculation and told her hurriedly:

'If the worst comes to the worst, I'd be pleased to have you stay with me,' and as her sister looked at her, her eyebrows ascending, 'I know how hard you work, but you could have the bed and I could put up a camp bed until you can find something.'

'Do me a favour,' said Christine sarcastically, causing Jemma to blush uncomfortably. She had no need to elaborate the point, and Jemma got to her feet to go to bed knowing that while she herself might not think the area in which she had her flat was the crème de la crème, her sister wouldn't be seen dead coming out through the front door.

'I'm sorry,' Christine apologised, seeing her acid remark had hurt Jemma's tender feelings. 'I'm just so worried I hardly know what I'm saying.' She then sent her a smile of such regret that although it still hurt that she could be so disparaging, Jemma just couldn't go to bed without making friends with her.

'Shall I make you a hot drink before I go to bed?' she offered.

'We're out of milk,' Christine declared.

The next morning Jemma got up early, and after washing donned her jeans and loose shirt, then raced to a near-by shop that seemed to sell everything and picked up a pint of milk and a paper, then hurried back to the flat only to find that Christine was up, but hadn't got time for so much as a cup of coffee. 'See you,' she said carelessly, and dashed off to her photographic session.

Jemma wasn't sure when she would see her next. From today she would be in full-time occupation of her flat. The thought was satisfying; she wouldn't allow herself to be homesick, she had already written to her parents. Perhaps she would write again tonight. And thinking of occupation, she had better start looking for that job that was going to make her one of the world's career women!

Slowly sipping her coffee, she scanned the situations vacant column of the paper she had bought, marking with a felt pen one or two possibles. And then her eyes alighted on one very promising advert that said, 'Junior secretary required by a growing firm of construction engineers, every prospect of advancement, only career-minded persons to apply'. It looked the very thing, and she felt a flutter of excitement grow within her as she noted down their phone number and thought, this could be it. This could be it!

She left making her phone call until she thought the first bustle of the day would be over. Then, instilling herself to be cool, calm and efficient-sounding—the way she thought a career-minded person would—she picked up the phone and rang Holden, Smythe and Partners.

'Mr Smythe will see you on Monday at eleven,' said an

equally cool, calm and efficient-sounding voice at the other end.

'That will suit me quite well,' said Jemma with detached politeness, only just saving herself from saying a happy, 'I'll be there!'

She had to grin as she replaced the phone. She was going to get that job. Well, if the competition wasn't too strong, she was, she qualified. She then went to tidy round Christine's bedroom, her unmade bed giving evidence of her hasty departure. Then she went to the bedroom she was using to pack her overnight things. She was in the act of stripping her bed ready to fold the sheets and take them to be laundered, when the thought suddenly occurred to her that while the clothes she had worn to work in Elvington were always neat and tidy, they weren't really smart enough for a junior secretary on her way up. On her sightseeing tours of London she had seen other secretaries leaving their offices at lunch time looking smart and 'with it' in their trouser suits, grey worsted, brown linen, even some with ultra-smart hats perched on their elegantly styled hair. She had her last month's salary in the bank, didn't she, her own savings, and the money her parents had given her, not that she would touch her nest egg, but why not . . .?

Five hours later Jemma was sitting in front of a large mirror while the skilled assistant behind her was blow drying her newly cut, shampooed and restyled hair. Her good fairy must have been with her the whole of this day, she thought, as she sipped the refreshing cup of tea one of the juniors in the busy salon had brought her. It had been the sheerest good fortune when she had bumped her way through the door with her many parcels purchased earlier that someone was ringing up belatedly, cancelling an appointment due in ten minutes, and that she had been able to take it. She seldom visited the hairdressers having no trouble in managing her thick hair herself, and it was the first time she had had a man attend to her hair. But she had been quickly lost in admiration for his skill when after giving him the barest instruction, 'I want a new style that will suit my face and be easy to manage,' he had set to with a speed that took her breath away, and great hanks of her hair had fallen from her head entirely unmourned by him.

She had no idea what this final splurge to her new image was going to cost, but it hardly seemed to matter in view of the gigantic spending spree she had been on. That lemon trouser suit had been irresistible, she thought, as had been that green two-piece. The long dress had been an extravagance since no one wore long dresses to work, did they? Of course they didn't. It had to be admitted she was a greenhorn, but she'd learn. She hadn't stopped at the outward trimmings either, since she had always been brought up to believe that what went next to the skin should be as respectable as what went on top. Really, she considered, if she had been buying her trousseau she couldn't have made a better job of it. She felt a slight twinge of guilt at that thought because it brought Oliver to mind, then consoled herself that she hadn't known he was going to ask her to marry him had she? And anyway, why shouldn't she have lacy undertrimmings if she wanted them. The extravagant bug had really been with her, and having witnessed, with some fascination it had to be said, the way Christine sat before her dressing table mirror for at least half an hour before she went out on a date and applied her make-up in a way that any artist could be proud of, Jemma had splashed out and bought new eye-shadow, mascara and a new lipstick.

'How's that?'

She was brought back to the present by the man standing to the side of her inviting her to admire his handiwork.

'It doesn't look like me!' she gasped. Then studying as she was being bidden the way her hair had been cut to hang in a gleaming curve just below her nape, a flick of a fringe swept to the side of her face, she gasped again. She didn't look ordinary any more, she looked—she took a deep breath —she looked eye-catching. She shook her head in disbelief, then stifled a moment of fear that she had spoiled what he had done, then relaxed as her hair bounced right back into place.

'It's beautiful,' she said, with such obvious sincerity that the hairdresser smiled back at her and her compliment to his skill.

'Correction,' he said. 'You are beautiful.'

Jemma left the salon clutching her various parcels, sure that everyone was looking at her. They weren't, of course, everyone was much too busy going about their own business. Though when she heard a wolf whistle behind her she was sorely tempted to look round and find out if it was for her.

Inevitably, it seemed, cluttered up as she was with so many parcels, the paper carrier of the first of her purchases that day, having been much picked up, put down and changed from one hand to the other, began to give way. When the handle finally tore in two, she had to stop and adjust all her other parcels. The obvious thing to do was to find a taxi, but being unused to flagging down a taxi and knowing she would feel a complete and utter fool if it sailed on straight past her, she stood for a moment wondering what best to do before realising Christine's flat wasn't so very far away. Then as she remembered she had left the sheets she intended to take to be laundered in the flat, her mind was made up for her. She would go to Christine's, transfer all her things into one of Christine's suitcases, leave her a note saying what she had done and return the case when she brought the sheets back.

Once inside Christine's flat, she took all her things into Christine's bedroom, took down her largest suitcase, then collected her nightdress and the sheets and set about transferring everything into the case. She thought perhaps she would wear the green suit for her interview on Monday. It was rather a lovely thing and would boost her confidence no end. About to pack the lemon trouser suit, she couldn't resist trying it on, first snipping off the price tag to get the full effect without the tag dangling down the front. A sigh of pure satisfaction escaped her as she stared in wonderment at what new clothes and a new hair-style could do for a girl. Then she found she was much too feminine not to have gone so far with her new image without experimenting with her new make-up—not too much though, she hadn't Christine's flair for putting a lot of make-up on without it looking too obvious. A suggestion of a smear here, a touch more mascara there, now for her new lipstick. Good heavens, what a difference! Her own mother and father would do a double-take if they could see her now.

It wasn't often vanity got the better of her, but so delighted was she with the person who looked back at her, she just had to have another look. And then the door bell rang, causing her to halt in her inspection. She checked her watch. Good grief, five o'clock! Perhaps it was Mark come to see Christine. There had been no need to ask her what time she would be in since she hadn't anticipated being here when Christine got back; perhaps she was finishing early tonight, only Mark had got here first.

Wondering if he would greet her with the usual. 'Hello, green eyes,' as was his habit, though expecting she was in for some of his teasing if, since he had eyes only for Christine, he recognised the change in her at all, Jemma went to answer the door.

She wasn't greeted with 'Hello, green eyes,' or any other teasing remark. In fact the man standing there looking casual in a fawn sweater and cavalry twill trousers, when she had only ever seen him before in business suiting, said not one word as he surveyed her from head to toe, and she was sure of one thing, he was in no way impressed by what he saw. The hairdresser had said she was beautiful, and his comment had warmed her, but the look Karn Fellingham was favouring her with told her as if he had spoken that in his view beauty came from the inside—he was not as impressionable as her tonsorial expert.

'I see you've been out on a job,' he said coldly. Then, his coolly appraising look going over her once more, 'I have something else for you to do. I think you will consider it worth your while to comply with what I have in mind—I'll come in.'

The sheer audacity of him! 'No, you won't,' Jemma said hotly, coming to life quickly at his calm statement that he would cross over Christine's threshold. He had been inside this flat twice before, and neither time had been very pleasant. 'You can say what you have to say right there,' she added, not intending to budge an inch other than to close the door on the most horrible man it had been her misfortune to meet.

'Even if what I have to tell you could mean you won't have to give up this flat?' he asked, seeming to have no doubts at all that that one simple sentence would gain him admission.

Jemma's inclination to slam the door in his face was forced to take a back seat. She had no idea what method he could use in getting Christine's landlord to renew her lease, but for her sake, her own inclinations had to be held down. Christine would never forgive her if she let even the smallest chance go of retaining the flat.

'You'd better come in,' she said begrudgingly.

'Thought that would get you,' said Karn Fellingham insolently. 'Always were a girl who knew when to give in graciously, weren't you, Miss Nokes?'

CHAPTER FOUR

JEMMA didn't invite him to sit down. Her brain was doing some rapid thinking as she turned and faced him as soon as she heard him close the door. He knew through Mark that Christine was under threat of having to give up her flat, but if his saying that he knew a way of her keeping the flat was just some ploy to gain him admittance so that he could have another go at her about his nephew, then she would very soon show him the door, as big as he was.

'You said something about this flat,' she reminded him when he just stood watching her, 'or was that just one of your endearing little ways of getting in?'

He ignored her sarcasm. 'Mark came to see me this morning. At the risk of stealing his thunder, I'll tell you he intends to ask you to marry him when he sees you tonight.'

'Does he need your permission to do that?' Christine would be in the seventh heaven when Mark proposed, but Mark took a slight dip in Jemma's estimation that he wasn't man enough to ask her to marry him without first getting his uncle's blessing.

'No,' Karn Fellingham told her evenly. 'Mark can marry whom he pleases, he has no need at all to consult me.'

'Then why ...?' she began, only to receive some of Karn Fellingham's own particular brand of sarcasm as he broke in rudely:

'Dear me, Miss Nokes, I was under the impression you knew it all. Surely you haven't forgotten that until Mark leaves university—if he ever does pass his exams while he's dancing attendance on you—he is completely reliant on the financial support I give him?'

61

She had forgotten, purely because it wasn't in any way important to her. To Christine either, she thought, but now it was coming through that if Christine and Mark were to marry before Mark finished university, then they would have to depend on what Christine earned to keep them until such time as Mark was able to get a job. Well, other students did that, she was sure.

'So Mark came to you and asked you not to cut off his allowance once he was married?' she asked.

Karn Fellingham shook his head, his look cynical. 'No such thing. He has no idea how I regard you, Jemma Nokes, has no idea of how much I know about you—and your relationship with him other than bed can't be as close as all that, because you've never breathed a word to him that I've called at this flat on two previous occasions.'

Jemma ignored his remark about bed, it was typical of the way his mind would think. 'So if he didn't come to see you about his allowance, then why else should he come and tell you he intended to ask—me to marry him?' She had nearly slipped up there and said, 'ask Christine to marry him'; she'd have to watch every word she said to this man, he was much too sharp not to pick her up straight away on the smallest slip she made. Though why she was still pretending to be Christine she had no idea, other than perhaps that of keeping her sister from receiving the blunt end of his tongue. 'Surely Mark doesn't hold you in such affection that he wanted you to be the first to know?' she jibed when Karn Fellingham showed no sign of answering her previous question.

He ignored that altogether, and dug his hands deep into his trouser pockets as though saving himself from wrapping them around her neck.

'You're an expensive lady,' he said shortly. 'Mark confessed he hadn't got round yet to acquainting you with his lack of finances.' He looked puzzled for a moment before continuing, 'Had I not told you personally that he hadn't two ha'pennies to rub together, I would have thought you were still labouring under the impression that he had a horn of plenty.' Jemma refused to say anything to that. She hadn't told Christine that Mark was penniless, but she still thought it wouldn't matter to her anyway. 'Mark didn't come to me to ask me not to cut off his allowance,' Karn Fellingham went on. 'He came to ask me, should you do him the honour,' the word honour came out sneeringly, 'of becoming his bride, if I would double the amount he receives from me at the moment.'

Jemma swallowed down her surprise. 'Knowing whom he has chosen to be his bride, you refused, of course?'

'No,' she was informed, and realised he was far cleverer than she had supposed when he went on, 'The last thing I want is a family rift over some worthless female. But anticipating that you hadn't taken my word for it that the boy is broke, I made him give me his word he would tell you his true financial position before he made an offer for your *dainty hand*.' Sarcastic swine! 'Should you then accept his proposal, I told him I would do as he asked and increase his allowance.'

Jemma changed her mind about him being so very clever. Christine would listen to everything Mark told her, and it wouldn't matter a hoot that he was broke. And the very devil grew in her at Karn Fellingham's assumption, purely on the evidence of gossiping scandalmongers, that her sister was mercenary. So certain was she that Christine would accept Mark like a shot, she just couldn't resist the urge to attempt to try and see Karn Fellingham's cool savoir-faire disintegrate.

'When Mark asks me to marry him,' she said, her voice fairly tinkling with an ice of its own, 'as I believe I've told you before, I shall eagerly accept his proposal.'

Her effort to crack his king-of-the-castle manner was en-

tirely wasted, she saw that—though she wasn't sure what
to make of the narrowing of his eyes as he looked back at
her. There was a shrewdly calculating look on his face she
wouldn't trust as far as she could throw a grand piano. It
had all her instincts clinging together, urging her to change
the subject, and fast.

'A-anyway,' she said, beginning to feel agitated suddenly, her sixth sense telling her he wasn't prepared to leave
the matter there, 'I—I didn't allow you in to talk about
Mark and . . . and me. You said something about this flat—
or was that purely a ruse so that you could come in and have
another dig?'

'Ah, the flat,' he said, as if he had only just remembered
it. 'I should have mentioned that at the outset, shouldn't
I?' and he was being too polite, she thought, for the Karn
Fellingham she knew to be being sincere.

'Mentioned what?' she asked warily.

'That this flat has been sold. You have a new landlord
for the few weeks remaining of your lease, Miss Nokes,' he
said, looking as if nothing had given him greater pleasure
than to be able to tell her that. But the look on his face told
her he had an even greater pleasure to come, and she just
knew the answer even before she asked the question.

'Do you know who the new owner is?'

His smile didn't light his eyes, but his teeth gleamed in
a devilish smile as his lips parted. 'Would you believe that
I am?'

Jemma turned away. Yes, she would believe it. The real
reason why Christine's landlord wouldn't renew her lease,
she realised then, had been because he had been hoping to
sell the flat. A property in this part of London wouldn't
come cheaply, but why had Karn Fellingham bought it?
Especially knowing Christine was the tenant? And there
Jemma had her answer. Her sister had had very little
chance of having her lease renewed by her old landlord.

With the new landlord, pigs would sprout wings before her lease would be renewed.

She turned back to him, her dislike evident. 'So what you really came here for was to be able to tell me and gloat,' she said disdainfully. 'Well, now I know. Perhaps you wouldn't mind leaving.'

'Mark tells me that you're desperate to keep this flat on,' Karn Fellingham said, not yet ready apparently to remove himself. 'I believe I said at the outset of our little discussion that there might be a way that could be achieved.' He paused, so very sure of himself that Jemma wanted to hit him. 'Do you still want me to go?' he asked smoothly.

Damn him! For herself she'd sleep on the pavement before she listened to another word he had to say. But the remembrance of Christine as she had been last night, pacing up and down, worried out of her mind because she so badly wanted to keep the flat on, forced her own instincts to be ignored.

'You're not giving anything for nothing,' she said bluntly. 'What is it you want?'

'Which is the more important to you, this flat or Mark?' he countered.

'Mark, of course,' she came back promptly, as she knew Christine would. Although they would need somewhere to live if they decided to marry straight away, surely that point was secondary.

She knew he was watching her closely, knew that he did not believe her and was infuriated that when he had aroused her curiosity he should remove his hands from his pockets and make every appearance of leaving.

'In that case,' he said, not taking his eyes from her face, 'there's nothing more to be said.'

He made to move towards the door, and the lightning flash of thought hit Jemma that this was one visit of his that she just couldn't keep quiet about to Christine. She would have to know he was her new landlord, and once she began to tell her about this conversation, Jemma was suddenly sure Christine would not be at all pleased if she hadn't found out what the particular carrot he had been dangling had been. His hand was on the door handle before Jemma found her voice, and a fresh wave of hatred for him broke over her so that she had to say:

'Just a minute.'

He turned, not troubling to hide the light of triumph in his eyes. It was clear he thought she was so desperate to keep the flat she would give up Mark.

'Changed your mind about Mark's importance to you?' he queried sardonically. 'Are you beginning to have doubts that I might be speaking the truth after all and that Mark really is without means?'

She wanted to tell him to go to hell, but certain that was his ultimate destination anyway, she decided against wasting her breath when his damnation had already been plotted.

'You want me to give up Mark in exchange for a new lease on this flat,' she said, stating what her rapid thinking had come up with.

'I have a new lease here already made out,' he said, dangling what he must think was a whole bunch of carrots as he extracted the parchment-looking paper from his back pocket that had been concealed by his sweater.

Changing her mind about telling him where to go, and about to do just that, another thought occurred to her. 'What's to stop me taking up with Mark again once I have that lease safely in my possession?' She wished she had thought before she'd said that. In her view Karn Fellingham and his nasty mind didn't deserve straight dealing, but the honesty in her that was as much a part of her as breathing had the question leaving her lips before she could hold it back.

'The thought had crossed my mind that you weren't above pulling a stunt like that,' he told her, endorsing for Jemma, if she needed it, that he had little or no opinion of her sister.

She held down her anger against him as the awareness came over her that if there was a way of getting that lease from him, then she would take any insult from him that he cared to throw. After today she would be in her own small flat, she'd post the sheets back to Christine if need be; never again would she put herself at risk of coming into contact with the most obnoxious man it had ever been her misfortune to meet.

'You planned for that, of course,' she said at last, speaking what she suddenly knew to be the case.

'Naturally. I'm not as gullible as Mark. And though you're a beautiful woman——' he saw her start of surprise that he should think her beautiful, 'oh, I've eyes in my head, Jemma Nokes, but I long ago discovered that beauty of face and body don't always go hand in hand with a beautiful mind and spirit.' The thought struck her that he had done his research on beautiful women in some depth, but she had no time to dwell on it, for he was continuing, 'Unfortunately, from whichever angle I look at Mark's involvement with you, I can't see any way he's going to come out of this without being hurt. That being so, I've decided that to force him to realise he has no future with you in one short sharp thrust will be much better for him than to have him wondering if perhaps there was still some chance for him with you.' He smiled that cynical smile that wasn't a smile. 'I'm sure you would turn down his proposal so regretfully that he would still be in some doubt whether you meant it or not. You'd love to keep him dangling, wouldn't you? But whatever other weaknesses he may have, Mark has more than his fair share of pride. Once what I have in mind has been put into action, I'm certain you will never see him again.' His eyes swept over her and he added with deliberate insolence, 'Mark isn't the type to want another man's leavings.'

Never had Jemma been spoken to in such a way, and nausea fought with anger even though his words were in actual fact aimed at Christine. But on the point of giving way to her anger, the vision of Christine as she had been last night came into her mind again, and stayed there. If only there was some way she could get back at him, some way in which she could make him eat his words—or failing that, some way in which she could turn the tables on him. Having gone so far in this charade, Jemma knew she was not now going to reveal that she was not Christine. Knew too, much as she would like to let go the rigid control she was exercising on her temper, she would not do so. When she related this whole sordid scene to Christine she wanted to be able to tell her everything Karn Fellingham had in mind, then should he at some future date try his hand again at splitting up her and Mark, she would know exactly the type of man she was dealing with.

'And how exactly do you propose to show Mark, should he and I get back together again when that lease is safely in my possession, that he will be marrying someone else's leavings?' she asked. 'Since I've been dating Mark there haven't been any other men in my life,' she was certain of her facts there, 'and Mark is man enough to know that any boy-friends I had before him don't count.'

She knew from the contemptuous look Karn Fellingham threw her way that he thought her mealy-mouthed and had substituted 'lovers' for the word boy-friends, and her whole body tensed with the effort of not giving way to the feelings that look aroused. If she lost her temper she would say much too much, might even reveal she was not Crysta-bella.

'I don't intend to show Mark anything,' he told her

coldly. 'You, Miss Nokes, are going to do that.'

'Oh ...?'

He ignored her querying word, and like a man whose patience had suddenly run out, he grated, 'The choice is yours—this flat or my impecunious nephew. And since I know you're a girl who likes to play both ends to the middle, I'm going to make sure you stand no chance of cheating. So you can quit stringing it out while your scheming brain plots the best way to have the penny and the bun. We both know you have no use for a penniless husband,' and then, a terrible coldness in his face, he told her what she had to do if she wanted the lease he was still holding in his hand. 'You are going to write a note to Mark telling him you are in love with someone else and have gone away with him. As I've said, Mark is going to be hurt, but he won't want you back once he knows you've been to bed with someone else.'

'Bed with someone else!' Jemma echoed, her anger disappearing as those words, some of her colour disappearing with it.

'You've gone pale, Miss Nokes,' he drawled, sounding in no way affected by her pallor. 'Unused to being backed into a corner with no way out, are you?'

Her backbone stiffened at his jibing sarcasm, and her anger came rushing back as she realised he couldn't be serious about her going to bed with anyone.

'Presumably, since Mark will not believe such a letter without coming here to find out for himself, I take it I'm to disappear somewhere for a while. Aren't you afraid I shall come rushing back to the flat once your back is turned?'

'Why should I be afraid?' He broke off, a definite glint of a man who has overlooked nothing coming to his eyes. 'When you disappear, Miss Nokes,' he announced, 'I shall be coming with you.'

Her gasp was audible. 'You mean ...'

'Yes, dear Jemma,' his voice was loaded with saccharine, 'I shall be the man you've fallen so heavily in love with. You and I will be going away together.' He paused to give her a lofty look. 'How does that grab you?'

'You can go to hell!' she spat furiously. My God, she thought, what sort of a mind has he got?

While her head was still reeling under what he had just said, her stunned eyes saw him calmly place the lease back in his hip pocket. 'That's your answer, is it?' he said, his manner telling her he had never wanted her for a tenant in the first place. 'It would appear you've just lost on both counts,' he told her, and, her brain slowly coming alive again, she realised he was still under the impression that once Mark had told Christine that he hadn't any money, then their romance would be off. So in Karn Fellingham's opinion, not only had she lost what she had thought was a wealthy suitor, but she had lost the flat as well.

And then Jemma's fury threatened to consume her. Just who the hell did he think he was that he could calmly stroll in here, calmly docket Christine as the biggest gold-digger of all time, and just as calmly set his calculating mind to work on breaking her sister's heart? Never had Jemma needed to control her fury more than at that point, and with her brain working overtime she checked the almost unsupportable urge to physically set about him. Breathing deeply, she noted he was favouring her with a despising look before he went to the door. And it was as he reached it, that her control came, and she found her voice.

'Wait!' she called, when he would have opened the door and gone through.

'Got all your conclusions neatly tied up?'

She ignored his reference to what he thought was her calculating mind, though she considered in this instance he wasn't so very far out. Her mind had been furiously busy in those few brief moments, and it had come to her that

with him believing her to be Christine as he did, then
should she do as he asked, and she had to own she found
the idea highly unpalatable, but if she did go with him—
and she reckoned she was just about angry enough to have
the courage to do so—then oh, the tremendous satisfaction
to be gained from outsmarting him! For, if she agreed, the
flat would be Christine's, and the love between her sister
and Mark would be totally untroubled. At this point her
stomach turned over at just contemplating going anywhere with Karn Fellingham, but she rode over the feeling,
and forced herself to ask the one very big question that had
to be asked.

She hadn't intended to clear her throat, but found she
had to before the question could be uttered. 'If I agree. If I
do go away with you . . .' she paused, the question sticking
in her throat, but she had to carry on, had to know, '. . .
then you won't—that is to say . . .'

'Either you're hoping for an Oscar or you have some idea
of making me believe you've never been away *alone* with a
man before,' he scoffed. 'Spit it out, Miss Nokes, spit it out.
I assure you I'm not likely to be shocked at anything you
have to say.'

Jemma glared at him. Oh, to be able to do him one in the
eye! Oh, the satisfaction to be found in not only securing
that lease for Christine, but to know she had put one over
on him and that try as he might he could do nothing to
harm the love of Christine and Mark. And once more,
stung by his scornful attitude, Jemma felt a return of the
ice-cold anger he had aroused in her before, and coolly,
without stammering or hesitation, she was then able to
complete her question.

'Should I decide to go away with you,' she said with a
coolness that amazed her, 'then do I have your word that
the arrangement will be platonic and nothing more?'

The answer he gave her was equally cool, though it hit

her as more cutting than cool. 'Contrary to the opinion you
have of yourself that your physical allure is more than flesh
and blood can stand, you can take any ideas out of your
head that I'll be bedding you this trip—there are some
lengths to which even I won't go. And,' he added, his tone
changing to stinging as he left her in no doubt that there
wasn't a trick in the book he didn't think her capable of,
'don't you start anything either. We both know you're a
push-over when the sex urge is stirred in you. Just remember this game is being played my way.'

Jemma's cheeks crimsoned, as much from his tone as
from what he had said, and she turned her head away so he
shouldn't see. It made her see red that he thought her
morals were that of an alley cat, and from the way he had
spoken, plain as a pikestaff, that if at any time during the
time he intended they should be away together he should
ever find his masculine urges too much for him, then he
would need only one look at her for any lust in him for a
woman's body to disappear. He thought her the dregs, that
was for sure. Well, that was all right by her, though she
had to brace herself against the sick feeling that knowledge
brought that anyone could think that way about her. But
with Karn Fellingham feeling that way, all she had to do if
she went with him was to stick out the ghastly nightmare
until he decided it was time to return. Ghastly nightmare
was an apt description, she thought, and then that thought
was followed by one that was almost beautiful in compari-
son. The thought that if she *did* go with him, who was
going to have the last laugh? Who? None other than yours
truly, that's who. It *was* a beautiful thought.

'How long will we be away?'

That she had more or less agreed to go with him was no
more than he had expected, she saw that clearly enough as,
his face expressionless, he said:

'I haven't decided yet.'

There was no arguing with that tone, she saw, but she tried just the same as she remembered her interview for her job on Monday. 'But—but what about my—career?'

His look told her he didn't give a damn about her career. Then, unbending slightly, 'Surely you can make a few phone calls cancelling your appointments? I'm sure you can think of something to tell your—clients.' Clients! He was making her sound like some call-girl. 'If it will make you feel any better, I'll promise to reimburse you for any income you lose.'

Trust him to think that money was the only thing that mattered to her. She shrugged the thought away there being other more important things to think about.

'When were you thinking of going?' she asked. She'd have to meet him somewhere, she didn't want to risk coming back here and for him to bump into Christine. Christine! Oh lord, she could come in at any moment!

'Now is as good a time as any,' he said laconically, taking all thoughts of Christine from her mind for a few seconds.

'Now?' she exclaimed, and received his cold unsmiling look.

'I believe I mentioned that Mark intends to propose to you tonight.'

Jemma stood as though frozen where she was until it came to her that having got her agreement, having stated he was ready to get off now, it seemed there was little else he thought he needed to add.

'You'll have to give me time to pack,' she hedged, thinking if she could only get him out of the flat it would give her a chance to write a note for Christine. Or, as the thought rushed in that at any moment Christine could come walking in through that door, she might be able to explain everything to her personally—if only she could get rid of him.

'That shouldn't take you long,' he told her, and with all

the easy assurance in the world he calmly sat himself down on the settee, showing every sign of sitting there until she had her case packed and was ready to go with him.

Without another word, Jemma left him. She went straight into the bedroom she had used last night, only to retreat rapidly as she remembered she already had a case packed full of all the lovely new things she had only just bought, in Christine's bedroom. That it had never been her intention that her new clothes should be worn to go away anywhere with Karn Fellingham was neither here nor there, she thought, as she took out the sheets she had packed and placed the jeans and shirt she had discarded in favour of her lemon trouser suit, on top of her case. These were the only clothes she had here, so they would have to go with her, she thought, while trying to come to terms with what she had committed herself to. But she mustn't think about it, there was no time. The important thing was to get out of here, and quickly. If she started having second thoughts ... She swallowed and concentrated on thinking about Christine. Heaven knew what would happen if she came home while they were still here. Jemma didn't hold out any great hope that she would be able to keep up this charade if that happened, or that Karn Fellingham wouldn't see for himself that of the two of them, Christine, coming in complete with her vanity box, wasn't more likely to be the photographic model of the two. As it was, if he ever found out about this deception Jemma was playing on him, then she had a fair idea he would set about separating her from her breath.

Wasting no time for him to tell her, as she was sure he would before they left, that there was still a letter to be written to Mark, she took the writing paper she had bought that day and with growing panic sat down and began scratching her head for something to write that, since she had every intention of signing herself Jemma, wouldn't make Mark think that Crystabella's sister had suddenly gone off her head.

Her letter took too many precious minutes to write, and she didn't waste any further time by placing it in an envelope and sealing the flap, knowing full well that Karn Fellingham would insist on reading it. Now to write some sort of explanation to Christine.

But before she had done more than pull the writing paper towards her again, a sound by the door had her looking up to see Karn Fellingham standing there. Impossible to write anything to Christine now, she thought, but she was glad she had thought to flick round her sister's room with a duster and make her bed before she had gone out on her spending spree. The only clutter in the room now was the pile of paper carriers she had discarded in favour of the suitcase, and she'd drop those off at the rubbish bin as they left.

Without waiting to be asked, she handed Karn Fellingham the note she had written to Mark, hoping he wouldn't want to waste any more time by telling her it wasn't to his satisfaction and ordering her to write it out at his dictation, though she thought it satisfactory herself. 'Dear Mark,' she had written, 'This will probably come as a surprise to you, but I have fallen in love with someone. I am going away with him. Forgive me, but I cannot go against my feelings. Jemma.'

Karn Fellingham handed the note back to her, commenting, 'I would think he'll be more shocked than surprised,' then, 'Why didn't you tell him I was the man you were going away with?'

So relieved was she that the fact she had signed herself Jemma, when Mark must always have referred to the

woman he loved as Crystabella or Crys, had gone un-
noticed, that she told him a thought that had been in her
mind when composing her letter.

'You said you were anxious to avoid a family rift.'

'And you care?' he asked, one black-as-night eyebrow
ascending.

'Mark is going to be hurt badly enough,' she lied, not
wanting him to have doubts about his opinion of her at this
stage, and thinking that Mark wasn't going to be so much
hurt by her letter but would, she hoped, think that since he
was so nearly a member of her family she had written to
him to break the news to Crystabella for her, for all no
mention of Crystabella had been made in her letter.

She placed the letter in its envelope and stuck down the
flap, and then lost any good marks Karn Fellingham might
have grudgingly awarded her—though she doubted she
had gone up any in his estimation—by saying, 'I can't remember Mark's address,' and when he gave her that dark-
browed look, 'Well, I've never been there,' and taking a
chance he didn't know any different, 'And since it's so
easy to pick up the phone and speak to him, I don't bother
with writing letters.'

At his dictation she wrote Mark's address on the
envelope, then had the envelope taken out of her hands.
'We'll post this on our way,' he told her.

Desperately anxious now to be away, the time going on
with every second bringing Christine's arrival nearer to
hand, Jemma left her seat, popped her writing materials on
top of her case and fastened it, then went to lift the suitcase
off the bed.

'When you make up your mind to something, you really
make up your mind, don't you?' he commented, and
when he made no move to get on their way and she just
stood looking at him trying to make out what was happening now, he said, 'I shouldn't have thought you would have

forgotten this,' and dipped his hand into his back pocket and withdrew the lease.

'Oh,' said Jemma lamely, 'I'd forgotten that.'

'Forgotten it?' he exclaimed, as if he doubted his hearing.

'Wh-what I meant,' she improvised hastily, 'was that I can see you're a man of your word. You wouldn't make me write that letter, go away with you and then go back on the arrangement.' She saw instantly she had said the wrong thing, though she didn't know why until he favoured her with a hard look, and said harshly:

'Cut out the flattery. It might get you everything you want with the Marks of this world, but just try to remember I'm immune.'

'Why, you conceited . . .' She broke off, hanging grimly on to her temper. There just wasn't time for her to give him a piece of her mind. But some time, some time between now and when he brought her back, he was going to receive what he had been asking for ever since the first time she had clapped eyes on him—both barrels!

She snatched the lease out of his hands. 'A copy of your old lease was handed to me on completion of my purchase of this property,' he told her, unconcerned whether she thought him conceited or anything else. 'I've had your new lease made out in your professional name since that was how the other one was made out.'

She wasn't particularly interested in the nuances she picked up in his voice that told her he thought Jemma was a perfectly sound name, being more interested in reading the top paragraph of the lease for a further two years between the landlord Karn Fellingham and the tenant Crystabella Nokes. Something about him told her it would be a fair and square agreement. Whatever else she thought about him, though she had no fixed idea why, she did believe that he wouldn't once everything else had been settled between them, try to put one over on her with hidden clauses in the small print.

It gave her a deal of satisfaction to prop up the lease on the dressing table where Christine would see it when she came in. And that satisfaction was boosted by a further satisfaction that bade her conscience be quiet, that Karn Fellingham wasn't putting one over on her, but by the dear Harry was she putting one over on him.

'You're not going to dissect every clause?' he asked, his brows coming together as though he couldn't quite make her out.

Her voice was pure syrup when she said, 'I'm sure you're much too much of a gentleman to put anything sneaky in that lease.' She knew her sarcasm wasn't appreciated, but he could be under no illusions that her words were in any way meant to be flattering.

He didn't answer her, she hadn't expected him to, but went and picked up her case. Good, all she wanted to do was get out of here, and fast. She picked up the jumble of paper carriers. 'I'll drop these off at the dustbins,' she said by way of explanation when she saw his eyes question what she was doing now.

After locking up the flat and dropping the spare key Christine had given her into her handbag, Jemma preceded Karn Fellingham down the stairs, willing herself not to race as was her instinct.

'I'll join you in a minute,' she told him when they reached the ground floor, 'the dustbins are through the back door.'

'I'm sure you won't object if I come with you,' he said suavely.

And only then did it hit Jemma that with that lease safely locked up in the flat, she had no need to go anywhere with him. But before that thought had time to take root, it was followed by another far less acceptable thought —that while it might look as though she was going with him voluntarily, she was in fact his prisoner and he was going to make certain she had no chance to escape.

CHAPTER FIVE

JEMMA had more than enough to think about as Karn Fellingham negotiated his highly powered car through London. It was quite all right by her that once he had seen her seated in his car he made no attempt to talk to her; she had nothing she wanted to speak to him about either.

His arm brushed hers when he pulled up at a pillar box and he reached over to the back seat to extract his wallet from his jacket. Jemma moved nearer to the door, not wanting the least physical contact with him. She saw the sharp look he gave her, but wasn't concerned by it, her mind busy with thoughts of escape. She watched him extract a stamp from his wallet and her heartbeats quickened. The instant he left the car to push that letter through the pillar box she was going to rocket out as well, and go like the blazes in the opposite direction. Christine's tenancy of the flat had been secured and if he drove straight back there to wait for her, the only person he would see would be Christine. Oh, it was just too beautiful! She could picture his bewilderment now when faced with the real Crystabella Nokes. And by now surely Christine had arrived home and seen the lease propped up on her dressing table. Knowing how badly she wanted that lease, it would take a better man than Karn Fellingham to get it from her.

'Here.'

Her thoughts were abruptly broken into, and the composed mask she had made of her features all but crumpled, elation at her thoughts dwindling fast as she turned her head to see him thrusting the letter towards her.

'Slip out and post this,' he ordered her.

'Me?' Jemma exclaimed, refusing to take it, her mind working double time—could she still make it with him watching her all the time?

'Is your rheumatism playing you up again?'

Sparks flew briefly in her wide green eyes at his sarcasm, but she conquered her ire, feeling defeated suddenly. 'Why can't you take it—it was your idea?' she reminded him, knowing she would stand a better chance in her bid for freedom if he turned his back on her.

'I don't intend to let you out of my sight,' he told her just in case she hadn't worked that out for herself.

'What's to stop me from walking to the pillar box and just keep on walking?' she challenged, though sprinting like the clappers was what she had in mind.

'I don't doubt there are many games you've played since adolescence passed you by,' he said coolly, 'but I doubt that rugby was one of them.'

Jemma stared at him, noticed then the very small hump on his otherwise perfectly straight nose, and knew from that that at some time he had been involved in a very tough game of rugger. Unspeaking she snatched the letter out of his hands, made to take her handbag with her, thinking he wouldn't be able to see her hands all the time and hoping to slip the letter inside her bag and make believe she had posted it. She corrected the opinion she had formed that it would take a better man than Karn Fellingham to outwit Christine. He was up to every trick in the book as he took her handbag from her.

'You won't need that,' he said.

She got out of the car and went unhurriedly to the pillar box. She had no wish to be brought down in a rugger tackle, being certain his long legs could run faster than hers, but she had no wish to return to the car either. Pushing the letter to Mark inside the mouth of the pillar box, she stood there undecided what to do. Then, her eyes going back to the car, she saw Karn Fellingham sitting there watching her, a look on his face that could only be described as anticipatory. That look telling her as though it was written in large print, 'Try it—just try it—it will give me the greatest of pleasure to flatten you to the concrete!'

Tight-lipped, she went back to the car, her temper simmering. If he said one word, just one cynical sarcastic word, when she took her seat, then she didn't hold out much hope that she wouldn't lose her temper completely, and regardless of the cost to herself, try to improve on what had been begun on his nose on the rugby field.

Karn Fellingham drove off without saying a word. Well, he didn't need to did he? she fumed. She was stuck here beside him until the car stopped. She was desperate to get away from him, realising too late that she should have been planning her escape back at the flat instead of worrying about Christine coming home and walking in on them.

But she hadn't known then that he would present her with the lease before they left, being sure he would hang on to it until after he brought her back from wherever they were going. She mentally kicked herself for overlooking that angle, for her lack of planning, but there had been nothing in her upbringing to prepare her for such double dealing. As it was she was stuck with him. The only redeeming feature being that with him thinking she was Crystabella, there was no way his plan to discredit her could work. She'd love to see his face when, as he was bound to do, he met her sister.

Jemma cheered up considerably as her mind took on a picture of Mark maybe asking him to be best man at his wedding. Her mind saw Christine in bridal white, the church packed, and with Karn Fellingham standing beside Mark waiting for the bride to arrive. Her fantasy went wild with delight at the shock and utter amazement that would be on Karn Fellingham's face when he saw a Crystabella Nokes he had never set eyes on before gliding down the aisle, herself behind as a bridesmaid ... At that point her fantasy came to an abrupt halt. Oh dear, if he went to the wedding, she wouldn't be able to go. Her imagination went wild again as she saw a picture of Karn Fellingham recognising her, of remembering the fast one she had pulled on him by impersonating her sister. She saw herself being picked up, being carried out of the church, satin and pink chiffon floating behind her, and of being dunked in the Elvington fountain, of being ...

'We'll stop here for something to eat.'

She was glad of his interruption; just thinking of ever coming face to face with him again once he was aware of the deception she was playing on him had made her insides tremble. She checked her watch. They had been travelling for over two hours and it had gone eight. She had no idea of their destination and she certainly wasn't going to ask only to be snubbed for her pains.

She stepped out of the car and saw he had pulled off the motorway while her mind had been busy with her thoughts. She looked around her. They appeared to have left the towns behind and were outside a country hotel. There were several cars in the car park; perhaps here was her chance to make a run for it. She might be able to get a lift. A lift to the nearest railway station would do. She wouldn't mind waiting all night for a train so long as she was away from *him*.

'Let's get it all said now, shall we?' his voice grated in her ears as she stood there looking in every direction checking for a place to hide if the need arose. 'We both know your cheating little mind has no intention of sticking to the bargain we made. But to save you using any further brain power, I'll tell you now. The only way you're going to get back to London and your flat is when I take you there. So forget any idea you have of appealing to the first likely man you see and coming on the frightened little girl act with those big green eyes. I'm up to anything you might attempt to put across, but should you make just one attempt to try anything, then by thunder, against all my inclinations, by the time I do return you to your flat, you'll be begging me for mercy.'

Oh dear, she didn't like the sound of that! His tone in itself, his anger barely controlled, terrified her. He wasn't joking, she knew that for a fact. But by the sound of it, what he would do to her if that remaining thread of control snapped would be to forget what he had said about there being some lengths to which he would go.

'I'm not hungry,' she said faintly, wondering where the girl had gone who had been looking forward to having the last laugh. 'You go in and eat, I'll just sit in the car.'

She might just as well have not spoken, for she felt his hand at the small of her back forcing her to go forward. She wasn't hungry, as she had said, he had just taken her appetite completely away. All ideas of making her escape left her then as she fought to beat the panic his tone and words had brought, that she truly thought she would have still been in the car waiting for him when he returned. Only that wasn't a chance he was prepared to take.

Without preliminaries they went straight into the dining room, Karn Fellingham, after one short look at her pale face, deciding to order for the both of them, and not endearing himself to her in any way when she saw that his appetite was in no way impaired.

'We have a long way to go,' he told her, looking up and seeing she wasn't interested in her food. 'Eat your steak.'

'I told you I'm not hungry,' she hissed at him, her agitation getting the better of her.

'Going on hunger strike, are we?' he mocked, showing how much he cared by returning to his own steak. 'Your figure is more shapely than I imagined most models' would be,' he commented carelessly. 'Perhaps you do need to lose a few pounds.'

Jemma glared at him. Although prior to her new wardrobe she had been inclined to wear rather shapeless garments, she had nothing to complain about in her figure. She had in her late teens, she recalled, worried for some weeks that she was perhaps a little on the lean side, and her measurements had altered not at all since then.

'Are you saying you think I'm fat?' she asked aggressively, and could have bitten her tongue as he looked up and gave her that sardonic smile that told her he had been trying to get her to rise and that she had neatly taken the bait. She saw his eyes go over the top half of her visible across the table, saw him take in her nicely proportioned breasts, and lowered her own eyes, feeling uncomfortable at his unhurried assessing of her shape, for all she had partly invited it.

'Would I be so ungallant?' he mocked.

If it wasn't for the risk of repeating herself, Jemma would have told him to go to hell; as it was she just ignored him and cut savagely into her steak, finding the first forkful and the next absolutely delicious. She had cleared her plate before she had simmered down enough to think calmly. And then it was to realise when it was too late to do anything about it, that if by his intimation that she was fat he had been looking for the perversity in her nature and thereby ensure that she had something in her stomach before they reached wherever they were making for, then he couldn't have done better. It irritated her afresh that he should have that touch of chivalry in him that decreed his prisoner should eat a hearty meal.

'Sweet?' he asked.

She would choke if she ate another thing. 'No,' she said surlily, and kicked against her upbringing that made her add the automatic, 'thank you.'

'Neither do I.'

He called the waiter over for the bill, extracted some notes from his wallet and stood up. Jemma followed suit. He didn't touch her as they left the dining room, but once outside, his hand came up to her arm and stopped her when she would have carried on to the outside door.

'The ladies' room is that way,' he said, nodding in the direction of an arrow that said 'Powder Room'. 'I shan't want to stop once we get going again.'

'I'm allowed to go on my own?' she queried, sweetly sarcastic.

'You're a big girl now,' he came back.

Very funny, she fumed, as straight backed she walked away from him. He was waiting for her more or less exactly where she had left him. And to anyone watching, there was nothing in the manner of either of them to show they would both prefer to have hundreds of miles separating them as he courteously held the door open for her to go through. Then they were on their way once more.

'Weren't you afraid I would do a bolt through the ladies' room window back there?' Jemma asked, having had time to think about it and becoming peeved at his odious confidence.

'Now that you mention it, the thought did cross my mind,' he said, and she could almost hear the smirk in his voice when he added, 'You'll forgive me, I know, for doubting your integrity, but the quick look I took outside showed that the windows from the ladies' room were no more than glorified air vents. Slender as you are, Jemma Nokes, even you couldn't have got through one of those.'

The annoyance she felt at his slighting reference to her integrity, plus the fact that had she chanced her luck and climbed through any window, then he would have been there waiting for her, was tempered by the knowledge that he didn't think she was fat at all.

'That reference back there to me being overweight was just so you could get me to react into eating my dinner, wasn't it?' she asked. Then, not needing an answer to that, 'Why did you bother? I would have thought you would have rejoiced had I collapsed through lack of nourishment?'

'Aside from the fact that I'd rather step over you than pick you up if you fell in a heap at my feet,' he answered, not pulling any punches, 'with what I have in mind for you, you're going to need all the strength you can get.'

Instantly alarm bells set off a cacophonous warning in her head. That was his second reference, she thought wildly, to what he had in mind for her when they reached their destination. Oh heavens, she hadn't got it all wrong, had she? He couldn't mean to ...? She hadn't blindly trusted him, had she, when common sense should have warned her, for all he had said ...

'Karn—Mr Fellingham,' she said in a rush, 'please, you said you wouldn't—didn't want to t-take me to bed. You can't ...'

'For God's sake,' his voice broke in harshly, 'what have I said? Do try to get your mind up above your navel and knock off that timid virgin act—I know differently.' Then, doing absolutely nothing to quiet her fears, 'I told you the idea of bedding you on this trip had not entered my head. That still holds good. Unless ...'

'Unless?' Jemma asked quickly.

'It's fast being brought home to me that I was right in my opinion before I'd even met you that you were a cheat of the first water. Even now your devious little mind is trying to think up a way of wriggling out of our arrangement. I'm not so unaware of what goes on inside your scheming head that I don't know that now you have that lease in your possession—a mistake on my part, I see now,' he added, 'I should have hung on to it until after this excursion is over. But you've made it abundantly clear by your furtive glances each time escape seemed possible that you have every intention of welshing on our bargain. So I'm telling you now that should you try and get away from me, I shall haul you back, and the conclusion Mark will draw from that letter you wrote, that you intend to have a holiday with the man you love, intend living with that man as though you were his wife for the duration of that holiday, will become a fact.'

A strangled gasp broke from Jemma. 'But you promised you wouldn't,' she accused. She had taken it as a promise anyway.

'And you promised, or so I thought, to keep to the terms of the bargain we made,' he told her heavily, pulling into the outside lane to overtake the vehicle in front. 'Break your promise to me, Jemma Nokes, and I shall act as I think fit.'

Jemma's stomach reacted as those words hit her. The dinner she had eaten turned on her, and nausea welled up inside that his threat wasn't being made just for the sake of it. What had come over her that time to react to his kisses the way she had done she couldn't think, but it was a certainty she would never be so weak again should he ever try anything like that again. She hated him, and would fight him every step of the way, she told herself, turning her back on the thought that he had been able to make her senses sing. As it was, she suddenly felt sick and defeated that what had seemed a wonderful way to get even with him back in Christine's flat was now showing every sign of being the ghastly nightmare she had first thought it would be. He was leaving her in no doubt that should he foil any attempt of hers to escape, then regardless of the cost to himself, he would exact retribution in full for her broken promise.

'Are you all right?'

Somehow or other he must have discerned that the weight of her thoughts were having a nauseous effect on her, for he was forced by a potential hazard up ahead to keep his eyes on the road. It had been dark for some time now, but it seemed even in the darkness of the car he was aware that all was not well with her.

'Perfectly all right,' she replied, her voice not as firm as she would have liked.

'Open the window if the pictures your imagination is conjuring up are affecting your stomach—I can't stop here,' he told her flatly.

'It is a little stuffy,' she said, and felt a morale-saving gush of air rush in as she opened the window wide.

Once the hazard had been cleared, Karn Fellingham pulled into the side of the road, stopping the car and switching on the interior light to turn and look at her.

'What is it with you?' he asked grittily. 'I don't personally kiss and tell, but I know of three men you've definitely been to bed with, so why this stomach hysteria at the thought you might, if you don't behave yourself, be adding to that number?'

He was making it sound as if Christine went to bed with just anybody, and she was just about sick and tired of his lies. At twenty-six, her sister might perhaps have thought herself in love before, might have gone to bed with some man. But from the way Karn Fellingham was talking, he thought Christine's heart had never been involved. Jemma searched desperately for some other excuse for her nausea, not seeing any reason why she shouldn't lie in return. He'd love it, wouldn't he, if he thought he'd got her scared sick?

'It has nothing to do with that,' she lied. 'I—I always feel car-sick after the first couple of hours of sitting in a moving car,' she pulled out of thin air. 'I ...'

'Why the hell didn't you tell me before?' he barked at

her. 'We could have found a chemist before we left London and got you something.'

Jemma began to feel better, especially since he seemed to believe what she had just told him. But she didn't trust herself to elaborate on the lie, unsure that he wouldn't see through the next lie she told him.

'Is that why you said you weren't hungry back there— because you thought your stomach would reject anything you sent down?'

'Yes,' she lied, and hoped he felt bad about it, though she thought it more likely he was thinking it served her right.

He looked at his watch. 'Ten-thirty,' he said, 'we should be there in another hour. There's nothing I can do about it now, but we'll stay here for a while until you feel better.'

'Thank you,' said Jemma, because she thought it was expected of her in this new invalid state. She had never expected him to be so considerate and felt a complete fraud, for all she suspected her stomach might act up again if she allowed herself to dwell on what he had threatened should she try and get away from him. The only thing to do, she reasoned, as Karn Fellingham looked ready to take advantage of their stop and take the opportunity to relax from his hours of driving—for all he had said when they had left the hotel that he didn't want to stop—was to see this thing through to the bitter end, that or risk having him as her lover. That thought had her head going to the window where she took in another lungful of air.

'Do you want to get out and walk about for a while?'

Really she couldn't understand this new side to him, but since if she got out and walked around she was pretty certain he wouldn't allow her to do so on her own, she refused the offer. 'No, thanks. I'm feeling much better.' Then since some of the edge appeared to have gone from his voice, and if anything he sounded not a little fed up, she asked the question she had decided nothing would make her ask. 'Am I allowed to know where we're going?' She had seen signposts with place names, but beyond thinking they were going in a south-westerly direction during the past hour, the whole journey had turned into a complete mystery trip.

'I'd have told you in London had you asked,' he said. 'We're heading for a small cottage I own on the edge of Bodmin Moor.'

'Bodmin? Cornwall?'

'The girl knows her geography,' he said with a return to his bracing sarcasm.

Jemma decided then and there she would never ask him another thing. 'I'm feeling better now,' she said tightly. 'If you want to get on, it's all right by me.'

He looked at her to see for himself if she was speaking the truth, then without another word being spoken he switched off the interior light, put the car into gear, and they were away.

He had said it was a small cottage. She knew what her idea of a small cottage was; two up and two down with a privy out the back. But would the description of a small cottage mean the same to him? Her mind went further and when he turned off the main road, passing through villages and then mile after mile of no villages at all, she was firmly convinced his moorside cottage would have at least four bedrooms, shower unit, the lot. And since he looked a man who liked his creature comforts, she decided he must have a housekeeper there and probably at least one other servant to wait on his every need. At that thought some of her tensions relaxed. She wasn't sure she had the nerve any more to try and make her escape; the deterrent he had in mind was ultimate, but with the thought of at least one other woman being in the house, she began to feel better.

When he turned the car on to a road that seemed to her

to be no more than a track from the bumpy feel of it,
Jemma wasn't particularly bothered. All she was interested in was the greeting they would get when the car
eventually stopped. Oh, it would be good to get away from
Karn Fellingham's solitary company! She reckoned it must
be around midnight by now, but she was convinced the
housekeeper would be up awaiting their arrival. The
ground beneath became even more uneven. Then after
several twists and turns, Karn Fellingham made one final
sweep of the wheel, drove on several hundred yards, and
there in the pitch blackness, its cold stone walls illuminated
by the car headlights, stood what Jemma could only
describe as a desolate, tumbledown shack that looked extremely sorry for itself in its complete isolation.

'Why have you stopped here?' she asked hoarsely, her
throat drying up and not wanting to believe what her brain
was telling her.

'We've arrived at our destination,' she was coldly informed.

'But-but,' she stuttered, then firmly pulled herself together, 'I'm not going into that—that—hovel!'

'You're sure as hell not sleeping in the car—I want you
where I can see you.' He made to step outside, leaving the
car headlights on to give them some guidance to the front
door, clearly not interested in any objection she had to
make.

'But where's your housekeeper?' she asked, knowing the
question was ridiculous. There wasn't a light to be seen
from the inside, and from what she could see of the size of
the place, if more than two people occupied it, then it
would be overcrowded.

Karn Fellingham stopped in the act of putting one foot
on the outside terra firma, and looked back at her, his voice
coming in mocking satisfaction at her obvious dismay.

'Now why would I need a housekeeper when I've

brought my own Cinderella with me?'

'Cinderella?'

'That's what I said. I think it's about time you soiled your lily-whites, Miss Nokes. Well, there's plenty of work to do here. The sooner we've finished, the sooner I'll take you back to London.'

Oh my God! Jemma thought, trying not to burst into tears. If the inside of this place was anything like the outside with what she could see of its neglected and wild-looking garden, then they would be here for months and months.

'You can't do this to me,' she protested, more concerned with the length of time it would take to get the place in order than the actual work involved.

'I can and I will,' he told her in no uncertain terms. 'You've had something like this coming for a long while. I'm only too pleased that I shall be the one to make you pay for all the nasty little tricks you've pulled in the past.'

'Nasty little tricks?' she echoed. Had he gone mad? He certainly was, she thought a second later, as he really let fly at her.

'I've checked up on you, Miss Crystabella Nokes, and none of what I've learned about you is to your credit. So desperate were you to get to the top of your profession you haven't cared a damn who you hurt on the way up—or whose bed you've slept in if you thought it was to your advantage. You have a cold, calculating brain, Jemma Nokes. You seem to have the impression that you only have to bat those over-long eyelashes nature has given you and every man will adoringly fall.' His harsh tone was shaking her foundations, but she wouldn't let him see it as he continued, 'Well, I'm telling you now, so there'll be no misunderstanding at the outset, that when the going gets tough you'll be wasting your time fluttering your lashes at me. I've got your number and you leave me cold. Now get out of this car and take your case with you, you can help me unpack the rest of the gear in the morning.'

Never had Jemma received such a dressing down. He had reminded her that he thought he was addressing her sister, and at that moment, if the fear hadn't suddenly come to her that he would kill her once he knew, she felt sorely tempted to tell him who she was. Her fear of what he would do to her won the day. He had already thrust her case at her from off the back seat and was already striding towards the door of the tumbled down cottage.

Her spirits lifted once she was out of strangling range, and she glared balefully at his departing back. Where was the man who had stopped the car when he had thought she was going to be sick? Where was the man who although he had wanted to get on had waited until she told him she felt better before driving on? He didn't exist, she realised. It came to her then that his only reason for stopping at all was because he didn't want her making a mess of the carpets and upholstery in his posh car should her stomach not have stayed under control. How he must hate her! All those terrible things he had said about Christine! But he couldn't hate her half as much as she hated him.

Hoping with all her heart that the inside of the cottage was an improvement on the outside, Jemma went to follow him. But she had gone not further than a few yards when she tripped on what she thought must have been a piece of rock jutting out of the ground, and measured her length among weeds, dirt and what must be gorse, since the hands she had put out to save herself stung painfully from the spiky impact.

She heard a muttered imprecation and found herself being roughly hauled to her feet, felt Karn Fellingham's hard chest against her, his arms round her for a moment as he steadied her.

'Don't *touch* me!' she said loudly, pushing at his wrist with her sore hands.

'From choice, lady, not with a disinfected bargepole,' he said rudely, then he took hold of her arm. 'Come on, I'm not standing here all night while you pick your way daintily to the door.'

His hand on her arm saved her from falling a further twice as each time she stumbled into him before wrenching herself away. But at last the door was reached and he pushed her through it.

Well, thank the lord it had electricity, she thought, as she stood blinking for a second, her eyes adjusting to the bright light coming from a shadeless bulb. But before she had time to do more than gasp at what met her eyes, he was saying grittily behind her:

'What have you done with your case?'

'I dropped it,' she replied shortly, and didn't care a damn that it was he who turned round and went out to look for it.

She went further into the room, a room that couldn't have seen soap and water for years. Cobwebs were hanging from every available surface. It was a kitchen-cum-living room, she decided, noting that there was a sink and a cooker along the window side of the wall, two cottage-type easy chairs pulled up to an empty stone fire place, a table and two kitchen chairs. A rickety-looking flight of stairs led straight from the kitchen to the room or rooms overhead and there was another door on the far wall. Jemma stepped over odd pieces of timber, new wood by the look of it, and went to open the other door to investigate.

The light from the kitchen showed the room to be a bathroom, but when she eventually found the cord to pull on the light, she saw it was a hastily constructed bathroom and thought it had probably been a pantry or something similar at one time. The cobwebs were less in evidence here at any rate, which was a blessing, but there was a bath there, small though it was, and with hot and cold taps too, but no wash basin. She flushed the lavatory that had an empty cigarette packet in it, more to see if the flush worked than to get rid of the packet. Water gushed out and she gave a small sigh of relief.

'I've had the plumbing and the electricity attended to—the rest we'll have to see to ourselves,' said Karn Fellingham behind her.

Unspeaking, Jemma backed out of the bathroom, unable to hide a shudder at the cobweb-festooned kitchen, even while knowing he was watching her closely, and no doubt ecstatic on seeing the revulsion on her face.

Her expression set, she looked at the rickety stairs. 'Where do I sleep?' she asked tightly.

Karn Fellingham stood to one side, drawing his hand back, palm open. 'After you,' he said, indicating she should climb the stairs.

'I would prefer it if you went first.' If there were rotting floor boards up there, she'd rather he went crashing through than her!

He gave her that sardonic smile she liked little better than she liked him, then went confidently up the stairs leaving her to follow. The first thing she noted, with something akin to relief as he switched on the lights, was that the stairs led on to a wide landing that had been adapted to make a bedroom. There was a bed there at any rate, as yet unmade, but piled high with blankets and other impedimenta. And the landing led into another room. He went through, switching on the light as he went. Jemma followed and saw another bed there with sheets and blankets piled on top. The linen looked fresh and clean anyway, she thought wearily, desperately looking for saving factors—that or go completely to pieces.

'This is your room,' she was told.

She walked past him and saw while the spiders had been busy here too, some attempt had been made to clear some of the cobwebs away. Someone had probably made a swipe at them with a broom, she thought. Then as she looked back to the doorway, her breath caught in her throat, and spiders became a secondary importance.

'There's no door,' she choked.

'That will save you looking for the key,' was the completely impassive reply.

Oh, he was a real little comedian, wasn't he! 'And I shall have to pass through your bedroom every ...' her voice trailed off at the superior look in his eyes. She clamped her lips together. That look told her as clearly as if he had spoken that should she take it into her head to try to creep out in the dead of night, then since she would have to pass his bed, notwithstanding that the stairs had creaked mightily when they had come up them, there was very little chance that she would be able to do so without him being aware of it. And if she was in any doubt about that, he confirmed it by saying:

'You might be interested to know that I'm an extremely light sleeper.'

Jemma ignored him, and seeing a wooden chair in the room, dusted it off with her handkerchief, mindful that her palms were stinging from her tumble, but gritting her teeth against it as she lifted the clutter off the bed, noted that the mattress looked clean and new and set about making her bed. She wished Karn Fellingham would go away, but he seemed quite happy to stand there watching her. In her haste to get the job done with, and quickly, so she could get into bed and possibly wake up to find this had all been some awful dream, she accidentally knocked one of her sore hands on the chair, and couldn't help the cry of pain that escaped her.

'What have you done?' he asked.

'Nothing,' she replied stiffly. But she could have saved her breath, because he had witnessed the small shake she had given her right hand when she had hit it, and he came over, taking her hand in his.

'You did this when you fell over?' he queried, and not waiting for an answer, picked up her other hand and inspected that too. 'You'd better go down and wash them thoroughly. There's soap and a towel on my bed,' he said. And when she would have ignored him and picked up another blanket ready to continue to make her bed, he added in an authoritative voice, '*Now*.'

Jemma looked at him mutinously. She had never felt so tired. All she wanted was to get into bed. Stubbornly she stayed where she was, then as his dark eyes narrowed threateningly, she turned her back on him and went into the room he was going to use, rooted among the blankets on his bed until she found the soap and towel he had spoken of, then went to the head of the stairs. She would have loved to have marched down them in none too silent protest against his high-handedness, but was not yet familiar enough with the stairs to trust entirely to their safety.

She noticed there were two suitcases by the cooker, hers and his, then applied her attention to filling the plastic bowl in the sink. That too looked clean and new, so she didn't have to spend any time in scouring it out first. She immersed her hands in water, heard the stairs creak, but ignored Karn Fellingham when he came and collected the suitcases. If he had come to check at the same time that his instructions were being carried out, then it didn't make her feel any sweeter disposed to him. Her hands felt better after she had bathed them, and since she had applied make-up—how many hours ago?—she felt too tired to even consult her watch, so she scrubbed at her face to remove every trace of make-up, leaving his towel hanging on the sink unit drawer to dry. Then gingerly she remounted the stairs.

He was just putting the finishing touches to his bed when she gained the top of the landing—well, thank goodness he hadn't expected her to make it for him. Jemma walked past without a word, then just inside her doorway stopped, surprise drawing her up short. The bed she had left only half made was now fully made up. She half turned round to thank him for doing it for her, then changed her mind. She had no idea why he had bothered; her hands didn't look that bad that he should have the idea making her bed would be painful for her, and if anything, she would have thought the idea of her being in pain would have pleased him.

She looked down at the trouser suit she had purchased only that day, and had difficulty in recalling the pleasure she had experienced at the time. And that was another black mark against Karn Fellingham, that he should have taken her earlier happiness away from her. Her hands went to unbutton her jacket, then froze. He hadn't said goodnight or intimated that he was turning in. She didn't think she had anything to fear from him so long as she kept to her side of the bargain; and of course providing he never found out she was Crystabella's sister. But since she didn't hold out any hopes that if he had anything more he wanted to throw at her that couldn't wait until morning, he would bother with the niceties of banging on the wall and waiting until she said come in, she just couldn't risk his coming in and finding her in a state of semi-undress.

Her hands dropping away from her jacket—she'd be asleep on her feet soon, she thought, exhaustion from the gamut of emotions that had raged through her that day fast taking over—she went to the doorway just as he was straightening up from his suitcase and saw her standing there.

She saw his eyes taking in her shining and scrubbed face, her eyes, unknown to her, wide in her face, her form wilting as she stood there, and she saw his mouth tighten the longer he looked. Hurried words left her lips before he could make any cutting comment.

'I'm—I'm going to undress now,' she stated baldly, when what she had meant to say was that she was going to bed. But if he thought the sentence had tumbled from her lips because the fear uppermost in her mind was that he would come in and catch her half naked, then he made no concession to her fear.

'Forgive me if I don't come in to watch—a strip show was never my sort of entertainment.'

Her tiredness left her briefly as temper shattered it away. Pummelling his head to a pulp was too good for him, she thought, knowing he would retaliate in kind if she tried it. Then control came to her and she turned back into her room.

She went to bed that night, tired, irritated, and utterly frustrated that in the absence of thumping his head, she didn't even have a bedroom door she could slam to give vent to her feelings.

CHAPTER SIX

IT seemed to Jemma that no sooner had she closed her eyes than there was a hand on her shoulder shaking her roughly awake.

'Go away,' she said, not yet ready to wake up and say 'Hello' to the world, her mind in a cosy cocoon of semi-sleep. She was even more unwilling when a hard voice informed her:

'It's time to get up.'

She knew that loathsome voice. All sleep fell from her, her eyes jerking open. Oh God, it hadn't been a dream! Karn Fellingham stood over her, impervious to the soft flush of pink on her cheeks. He was dressed in workmanlike trousers and shirt, and she didn't have to stretch her powers of imagination too far to know he intended she should get out of bed and act as his labourer.

'What time is it?' she asked, when he made no move to leave the room. She wasn't budging from this bed until he was out of sight.

'Six o'clock,' she was told. 'We have a lot to do today. Get up.'

'I will when you've gone.'

'Such modesty,' he said sarcastically, then gave her another sharp look when she stayed put. 'If you're not out of that bed in five minutes, I'll come and tip you out.'

'Such olde-worlde charm,' she bit back. Well, she didn't see why he should be the only one who could think he could be sarcastic.

'Five minutes or else,' he threatened, ignoring her jibe, and turned and strode to the doorway, ducking his head to pass under the lintel.

Jemma was out of bed as soon as she heard him going down the creaking stairs. Hurriedly she extracted her jeans and shirt from her case, then a delicate new bra and pants; was it only yesterday she had bought them?—it seemed aeons away. Then she was faced with a dilemma. It was second nature to her to wash before dressing, but with the bathroom downstairs, and in the absence of a dressing gown, if she was to carry out her lifelong habit, then she was going to have to go downstairs in her nightie. Distastefully she donned her clothes, pulled her bed open to air and went carefully down the rickety stairs, the smell of bacon frying coming up to meet her turning her stomach. In her view, six o'clock in the morning was too early to be eating bacon, or anything else for that matter. Well, one thing was for sure, she wasn't washing at the kitchen sink.

'Have you a towel I can use?' she asked his back.

'In the bathroom,' she was told.

It was too much to hope the bathroom door had a lock on it; it hadn't. Wondering if there was any hot water—washing in cold at six in the morning was just as bad as eating bacon, she considered—her spirits lifted to see hot water gushing out from the tap. She noticed a shaving mirror had been placed on the windowsill, saw her reflection looking tousled-haired and big-eyed and turned her back on it, noting as she did so that there were two fresh towels placed on the bath as well as soap. Toothpaste and Karn Fellingham's toothbrush were standing in a glass, reminding her she had forgotten to pick up her spare from Christine's. After her wash, deciding against a bath until she had cleaned the place up a bit, she used some of his toothpaste on her finger, brushed her hair, marvelling that it fell back into her new style without her having to fuss with it, then began to feel more like the Jemma Nokes who more often than not awoke in a sunny mood.

Her mind had been busy during her ablutions. There

seemed to be two of everything, two towels, two beds, two easy chairs, two kitchen chairs. It seemed to her then that Karn Fellingham had never intended to be the sole occupant of this remote cottage. And in view of its unkempt condition it didn't take much thinking about to know he had not had two of everything installed for one of the quiet weekends she didn't doubt he had with whoever was popular with him at the moment. She left the bathroom, her small flash of good humour disappearing, to see Karn Fellingham placing two plates of bacon and egg down on the kitchen table.

'I never eat bacon and egg for breakfast,' she said belligerently, which was a slight exaggeration.

'Suit yourself,' was the unconcerned reply. 'You have a lot of hard work to put in today—it isn't likely we shall be stopping for lunch.'

Jemma didn't like the feeling that she must be totally invisible as she sat down at the table and reached for one of the two mugs of steaming coffee she saw there. For Karn Fellingham was so intent on eating his breakfast he seemed unaware she was sitting there at all.

'You planned all this, didn't you?' she asked aggressively. 'You planned it every step of the way.'

'I don't like leaving anything to chance,' he replied, preoccupied with eating and obviously not caring a button that she was working herself up into a lather.

'There was a chance I might not come with you,' she argued, hating his smug complacency and feeling her palm itch with the desire to give him something he hadn't planned for.

'Hardly,' he said, lifting hard dark eyes from his plate to be entirely unmoved by the flashing anger in her green eyes. 'Once you smelt the scent of that lease, once it began to dawn on you that I might be right, might be telling the truth when I told you Mark hadn't a bean, and that there was a very big chance you might have backed a non-starter, there was no doubt in my mind that you would come.'

'But Mark only told you yesterday that he intended to propose to—me. You couldn't have got everything organised in such a short time,' she challenged.

'I saw the way the wind was blowing when Mark went over his head and purchased a bracelet he had no money to pay for. He's usually quite level-headed and would never do a thing like that unless some emotion was in charge of him that he couldn't control.'

'So you've been planning since then? You've just been waiting for Mark to confirm your suspicions, and then you went into action?'

'Something like that.'

Jemma was silent for a moment as she considered all he had had to do, and in a very short time, if his plan was to be successful. 'Did you already own this—for the want of a better word—cottage?' she asked.

'No,' he had no objection in telling her. 'The idea came to me when Mark told me you were desperate to stay on at your flat at all costs, but if the worst came to the worst, had I got anything going in the same area. He was extremely upset that his beloved might find herself out on the street. I thought then that if you were half as upset as him, then knowing your reputation there was very little you wouldn't do to keep your flat on. I asked Mark who your landlord was and when he told me, I realised I knew him, and also that he would sell if he could get a buyer.'

'So you bought the flat, decided on what my fate was going to be, then went out and bought this—desirable residence,' she put in disagreeably.

'So glad you like it,' he said with insincere charm. 'I just know you're going to *love* cleaning it up.' He got up and took his plate to the sink. 'Breakfast is over,' he announced. 'You can wash up while I bring the rest of the things in from the car.'

He went out, leaving Jemma to gaze about her, shuddering as she did so. He had said last night that she was to help him unload, but he must have changed his mind about that. She took everything off the table and dumped it on the draining board, and not seeing any washing up liquid, rooted around in the large cardboard carton he must have brought in earlier. But all she found there were tinned and packaged provisions, but no washing up liquid.

She ran the hot tap until it was scalding hot, then set to work, pretending he was as invisible when he came in as he on occasions seemed to think she was, as another cardboard carton arrived, then a broom, dusters and the like. Again she wondered how long they were going to be here, then looked down at her jeans knowing she was going to need a change of clothes and having no intention if it could possibly be avoided of wearing her new-image clothes to play Cinderella to his Prince Charming.

'Something amusing you?'

She hadn't known a whimsical expression had crossed her face at that last thought. 'Must be the trauma of these past twelve hours,' she said, biting her lip at the almost irrepressible urge to grin as she told him, 'I was thinking that I'm Cinderella, if you fancied yourself as Prince Charming.'

The opinion she had of him that he was an overbearing, arrogant brute was completed when she added lack of sense of humour to his other failings.

'As I remember it, Prince Charming fell in love with Cinderella,' he told her stonily. 'If you have any ideas in your head of turning this into a romantic interlude and thereby get out of pulling your weight, then think again, Jemma Nokes. You're here to work, so don't try and start anything you can't finish—you might get more than you bargained for.'

Jemma's indignation was riding high. 'For your information, Mr Fellingham, that disinfected bargepole you were
talking about goes for me too, only double!'

'Like hell it does,' he came back with rude scepticism.
'My one attempt to offend any sense of niceness in you
when I kissed you so roughly had you clinging on to me
like a limpet. I could have taken you then had I not known
I would have felt myself begrimed afterwards.'

Jemma winced at that. When it came to hitting below
the belt, he had no peer, had he? She opened her mouth to
attempt some defence of herself, only to find she was
wasting her time as, his voice icy now, Karn Fellingham
let her know in no uncertain terms exactly what she could
expect if she tried any of her wiles on him.

'I'm warning you now,' he told her, the coldness in his
voice making her want to shrivel up and hide, 'should you
try and come on with the sweet talk, the alluring glances,
then I shall make love to you in a way that will put you
off men for a long time to come.' He didn't wait to see what
she made of that, but went on, 'Try any of that with me
and you'll find out that I'm not some romantic young blood
with a care for any finer feelings that might be buried
somewhere deep down inside of you. Should we ever get
started on that bedroom nonsense, it will be touch and go
which one of us will feel more disgusted when I'm through
with you—so,' he threatened, his tone not a fraction
warmer, 'just don't you go starting anything!'

As a warning, he couldn't have rammed it home harder
if he'd used a pile-driver. Though it was something, she
supposed, that he had discerned that much about her to
suspect that she might have any finer feelings buried somewhere deep inside. But what he had said, the thought that
any of her glances might be interpreted as alluring, had her
too scared even to look at him. She had never felt less like
grinning now, and turned back to the sink so he shouldn't

see that, for the moment at any rate, she felt flattened.

'W-we need some washing up liquid,' she said, grasping at anything that would get him off the subject.

'I've got to go into town later. Make a list of anything else we need,' and just in case she had any idea in her head of making her escape when he had gone, he told her, 'I'll be taking you with me.'

After she had finished with the washing up, Jemma went upstairs, the temper that had deserted her while Karn Fellingham had been laying into her rushing in to lift her deflated spirits. Fuming, she made her bed and collected her writing pad. His bed was still unmade. She walked past it.

'Right,' he said when she joined him downstairs. 'It's roll your sleeves up time, Jemma Nokes.' He pointed to the broom. 'Get weaving with that.' Oh, to bring it down on his head! 'I have jobs to do outside. I want this place cobweb-free when I return.'

She glowered at him to no effect as he looked through her before turning and going out. He couldn't want the place cobweb-free any more than she did, but she wasn't going to be bossed around by him. She would do things her way, not his.

There were cupboards in the kitchen, and she would have liked to have given them a scrub with hot soapy water. But in the absence of soap powder, she liberally splashed water about and while the cupboards were drying, only then did she begin to tackle the ceiling and walls, grateful for the long-handled broom that enabled her to keep her distance from any livestock as she held back a shriek as two of the largest spiders she had ever seen objected to their habitat being disturbed and came out to investigate.

The kitchen looked far more presentable when she had finished, though it would need gallons of soapy water before she would feel comfortable there. The cupboards now dry, she found homes for the contents of the two cardboard boxes, then, not seeing why she shouldn't, made herself a cup of coffee and sat down to write her shopping list. Where Karn Fellingham had got to she neither knew nor cared.

At ten past nine he joined her, surveyed the work she had done so far, and opined, 'There, that didn't hurt, did it?' Then as though the word 'hurt' had fired his memory, 'Let me see your hands.'

'They're all right,' she said coldly, stung again by his sarcasm, but was forced to bring her hands out for his inspection as he just stood there silently waiting.

He looked her hands over, satisfied himself they were not infected and observed, 'They don't look as though they knew very much about honest toil.'

'Ever heard of rubber gloves?' she asked shortly, thinking of the way she had laboured in her new flat, the little flat that was growing dimmer and dimmer in her mind. She mustn't start to get anxious about returning to it, or her enforced stay here would become more unbearable than it already was.

'That's the list,' he said, taking up the sheet of writing paper that was full with the things they hadn't got, but which Jemma considered essential they should have.

He read down the items written in her neat hand, not commenting until he came to polish. 'Polish?' he said out loud. 'Ye gods, you are trying to make an impression, aren't you?' Jemma gave him a speaking look, then wished she had written the things she required for her own personal use on a separate piece of paper, as he read out, 'Toothbrush, shampoo, T-shirt, dressing gown. Dressing gown!' he repeated. 'Why not go the whole hog and get your new winter wardrobe while you're about it?'

'I didn't realise I was coming here to work,' she defended. 'I shall need a change of working clothes—I'm filthy already. And it may have escaped your notice that since I have to pass through your room every time I want to go to the bathroom ...'

'Say no more, we must preserve your modesty at all costs. We'll go now.'

Why she should feel mean she didn't know, because he didn't deserve any less, but her hard work having got rid of her ill humour, she found herself asking, 'Do you want a cup of coffee before we go?' After all, she had had hers, then she noticed he was giving her a hard look. 'Forget it. I wasn't trying to vamp you, just feeling guilty that I've had a coffee and you haven't.'

She stood up, taking her handbag from where she had hooked it over the kitchen chair, and felt his hard hand on her arm as she would have marched in high dudgeon to the door.

'You can make me a cup of coffee when we come back,' he said, some of the hardness going from his voice.

'Did I put weedkiller on that list?' she asked, and was absolutely shattered when he laughed as he caught her meaning that if she made him coffee when they came back, then she wouldn't at all mind putting a suggestion of paraquat in it.

'Leave your bag here,' she was instructed, the laughter gone from him.

She looked at him, a question in her eyes, before it dawned on her that he thought once they had reached town she would try to get away from him and make for the nearest bus or railway station. Without her bag and money, her chances of getting anywhere were minimal.

She banged down her bag and marched out to the car. She would liked to have changed, but settled for dusting down her jeans instead, having a feeling he would oppose any suggestion she made that he wait for her as being thoughts of pure vanity coming from the girl he thought she was.

It was midday by the time they had returned to the cottage, and never once had he allowed her to be on her own, taking hold of her arm when they were walking along pavements and going with her to buy a dressing gown. Jemma chose the cheapest one she could find, having a perfectly good one at her flat, and waited with every intention of paying him back while he paid for the tricel wrapper and received the paper bag from the assistant.

She took the things that were her purchases straight up to her room when they returned, calculated how much he had spent on them, then not having enough money to give him the cash she wrote out a cheque for the amount and dropped it on his bed, still unmade, on her way down the stairs again. By this time her tummy was rumbling noisily. Tomorrow, she decided, if she got the offer, she would eat every scrap of breakfast, but for the moment she was starving and she couldn't very well get herself something to eat without asking him if he wanted something as well. He seemed to have forgotten he had said she could make him a coffee when they returned.

She wondered if she should go outside and ask him about lunch, then heard the rattle of the door just before he came in carrying a hammer and nails and looking ready to do his carpenter bit.

'Were you serious about our not stopping for lunch?' she asked, hating to have to ask the question, but feeling she'd be fainting from hunger if she didn't eat soon. She watched to see if a smug look of satisfaction crossed his face, but he looked no more than passingly interested, his mind being on the task he had set himself.

'You can knock something up if you like,' he told her. 'Give me a call when it's ready. I'll be upstairs fixing the bedroom windows, it looks like rain.'

Jemma set to with peeling potatoes. Her bedroom window had remained open all night, the catch having long ago disappeared, she suspected. She had realised then that the rotting wood would have to be replaced with new before a new catch could be set in place.

Three-quarters of an hour later, the table laid for two, she went to the bottom of the stairs, waited until there was a lull in the banging, then shouted up, 'Karn!' sucked in her breath, and hastily amended it to, 'Mr Fellingham, lunch is ready!'

She kept her head averted when he came down the stairs and went to the sink to wash his hands. He came and took his seat. 'Lamb chops, peas, carrots and potatoes,' he observed. 'I don't recall buying a cookbook.'

That really was one time when she could give him a superior look. Anyone in her view could have cooked what she had without their efforts coming to grief. He might be able to handle a frying pan, but it would appear that Karn Fellingham just wasn't acquainted with saucepans.

'Just a little something to keep us going until dinner, Ka ... Mr Fellingham,' she said, not meaning to sound as smug as the words came out, and going pink that she had nearly called him Karn.

Her smugness disappeared when he commented, 'My first name seems to come easily to you,' squashing any smugness in her, and looking puzzled that the girl he thought her to be could blush at all, let alone at such a small matter. 'Why not use it?'

Jemma cut into her chop, glad she had somewhere else to turn her eyes rather than at him.

The afternoon progressed with a series of bangs and crashes coming from the floor above. Jemma attended to the washing up, then began putting away the shopping they had bought, coming across with some amazement a pair of kitchen gloves she hadn't see Karn purchase when pushing the trolley round the supermarket. So much for his talk about her soiling her lily-white hands, she thought, trying the gloves on and finding they were just her size. She paused to wonder how he could be so horrible to her most of the time, and yet occasionally do something that had the edge going off her hatred of him. Not wanting the invading thought that perhaps he wasn't as bad as she had dubbed him, she set about giving the bathroom a birthday, sweeping ceiling, walls and floor before getting to work with the hot soapy water she had promised herself on both walls and floor.

She had just washed down the walls of the kitchen and was deciding they would have to be done again to make a proper job of it, when Karn shouted down:

'Any chance of a cup of tea?'

'Right,' she shouted back, thinking it the best idea he had so far had, the thought coming to her that since he had disappeared upstairs he had made no effort to supervise what she was doing, and she could have been reading a book for all he knew.

'Do you want your tea up there?' she called, and was unsure of her reaction when he said he would come and join her.

'I need something from the car,' he said when he came down. 'Might as well have my tea before I go back up.'

He picked up his mug of tea, his eyes going round the room and noting the rubber gloves one on top of the other on the draining board. 'Been busy?' he queried, two lines of a frown furrowing his brow as he looked around, seeing the brown walls were now looking more of a dirty yellow.

'Did you think you'd have to crack a whip to get me into action?' she asked with some satisfaction. Clearly he thought she had never done a hand's turn in her life apart from push a vacuum cleaner around.

'You did a fair amount this morning before we went out,'

he said slowly, as though wondering what her motive was to have washed down the walls without him having to order her. 'I thought,' he went on, as if it was being dragged out of him, 'that your stomach might still be feeling queasy from the car ride last night, that you might need a rest this afternoon.'

'I feel fine,' Jemma said stoutly, guilt at her lie of last night upon her.

His eyes studied her face, saw she didn't appear to be suffering any after affects. 'In that case,' he said, placing his mug down on the table causing her to think his stomach must have an asbestos lining since he hadn't waited for it to cool before he drank it, 'you can have a go at the bathroom as soon as you've finished your tea.' The look on his face had grown hard, telling her he didn't trust her open expression when he knew so much about her.

'And after I've done that?' she asked sweetly, having already decided what her next chore was going to be and needing no help from him in getting herself organised.

'You'll have enough there to keep you going until it's time for you to start preparing dinner,' he said shortly, and left her to go out to the car.

He was back before she had urged her mutinous body to move. He came in carrying sandpaper and holding the toothbrush she had purchased that morning all neatly wrapped in its plastic covering. She realised it must have fallen from the carrier and on to the car floor, but before she could snatch it out of his hands he was striding past her to deposit it in the bathroom.

There was silence when he opened the bathroom door, and she sought for some bright remark to scorn him with knowing he would come back and ask why she hadn't told him she had worked hard to get the bathroom looking as immaculate as it ever would, given that it had an untiled concrete floor, was curtainless and didn't have a hook or a rail anywhere to hang anything.

The silence stretched. Jemma was aware he had come to stand looking down at her, and she lifted her head in defiance, saying airily, 'Didn't know I had a magic wand did you?'

'I don't get you,' he muttered. 'I thought I knew something about women . . .' and then some, she added silently. And then he made the connection she was sure placed her neatly into the right little box. 'You really are desperate to get back to civilisation, aren't you?' he said, and went back upstairs to continue his hammering.

Jemma, following his train of thought, saw that he didn't give her any credit for not wanting to live in a pigsty. He thought her sole motive in cleaning the place up was so that the sooner it was done the sooner they could go back to London.

The walls came up a brighter yellow after her second application of soap and water, and if in the process of getting rid of the grime that must have been on them for years, large chunks of plaster came away in her hands, then she thought that couldn't be helped.

Karn had finished his work upstairs and was now outside again. He came in, his arms loaded with wood which he placed in the fireplace, causing her to realise it would be cold later, and they would need a fire.

'Shall I start dinner now?' she asked, feeling more weary than hungry, but thinking she wouldn't be allowed to go to bed until she had fed the brute.

'You looked whacked,' he said, the pleasure she had expected to hear in that statement missing. 'I'll do it if you like while you take a breather.'

Startled by his offer, her eyes flew to his. She was sorely tempted to accept, but thinking once she sat down she might not be able to get up again; she had thought after redecorating her flat that her body wouldn't be able to

find fresh muscles to ache, but it had—she didn't dare
think what she would be like tomorrow.

'Wouldn't dream of letting you,' she said, ignoring the
narrowing of his eyes that she wasn't ready to stay in the
little box he had thought she slotted neatly into. 'Besides. I
enjoy cooking.' Now sort out what sort of woman I am!
she thought.

Karn didn't argue the point, but set about laying the
fire, and since he was probably famished after his physical
labours, Jemma pushed a fair-sized steak under the grill,
added tomatoes and set about fixing a side salad. He'd
have to manage with cheese and biscuits for afters, she'd
left it too late to think about making a pudding.

As she had suspected, he was hungry and made a much
better showing of eating his meal-than she did. But though
she was aware he was watching her, again he made no
comment. She had nothing she wanted to say to him and
he apparently had nothing he wanted to say to her. De-
pression descended on her. She tried to shake it off, knowing feeling tired didn't help, and forced herself to her feet
to do the washing up, only to find Karn had joined her at
the sink and had begun drying the dishes as she washed
them.

Her rubber gloves forgotten in her tiredness, she thought
there was something calming about having one's hands in
water, or so it seemed to her then. At any rate she wasn't
feeling any hostile impulses against the man standing near
to her. Her mind flitted from thought to thought until
suddenly, with a sense of shock, it came to her that she had
been thinking dreamily that this was what it must be like
being married. That she was married to Karn and that, the
evening meal over, he had come to help her.

The shock of thinking of him in any way completing the
picture of domestic bliss had her hands going rigid on the
plate in her hand. Good heavens, she had been in his sole

insufferable company for just over twenty-four hours now
—was having to put up with the situation she was in sending her round the bend? Of course it wasn't, she told herself sternly. It was just that, coming to this after the warm
loving relationship her parents had, the warm loving home
she had voluntary left, she was finding the contrast too
great. A sudden wave of homesickness hit her, and tears
sprang to her eyes before she could stop them. She was
totally unaware that Karn had ceased in his drying up and
was in fact staring at the unhappy expression on her face,
and she jumped, startled, when his voice, deep and not
ungentle, asked:

'What's the matter, Jemma?'

Had his voice been cold or harsh, she might well have
been able to conquer her moment of weakness, but it
wasn't cold or harsh, and she turned her tear-drenched eyes
to stare wordlessly at him. And then, hating like most
people to be caught in tears, she left her chores at the sink
and bolted for the stairs. She never made it to her room,
for as quick as she was, Karn was quicker, and he caught
her at the bottom of the stairs.

'I asked you a question,' he said, hanging grimly on to
her shoulders when she tried to break away.

Jemma stilled, looked at him, swallowing hard. She felt
juvenile, stupid even, but worse, she just couldn't get over
the feeling of wanting to howl her eyes out.

'Oh, Karn!' broke from her in a helpless groan, and she
had no idea then whether he pulled her or whether she
homed nearer seeking comfort, being the girl her mother
had said was a 'softie', and proving to be so by wanting to
be part of a happy family circle again and away from the
gloom of her present surroundings.

'What is it?' he asked, bending his head as though
suspecting her answer would be whispered.

How he would roar if she confessed she was just going

through the pangs of having cut her home ties for the first time, was going through an unexpected feeling of homesickness and wanted the warmth of someone loving her after so much hate coming her way.

About to pull away from him, suddenly she didn't need to. For as though he had just remembered he hated her and that to hold her in his arms had not been on his list of suitable punishments for the trollop he thought she was—providing she didn't send him any alluring glances—he pushed her away, though he kept his hands on her shoulders.

'If you're trying to pull a fast one, Crystabella Nokes . . .' he said threateningly.

The shock of hearing her sister's name on his lips brought Jemma round to what had happened in the last few minutes. For a full two seconds she was literally dazed to find she had been in his arms, had rested her head on his chest. Then, even while not understanding what was in the man that it had been instinctive for him to try and comfort her before his cool assessing brain had taken over, she shook his hands from her. The last thing he was going to hear from her was anything of her true thoughts.

'Nearly got you there, didn't I, Karn?' she jeered, forcing her natural feelings into the background. Her eyes felt moist and she wiped her hands, still damp from the washing up, down the sides of her trousers before wiping the back of her hand across her eyes. 'I should have thought,' she added, seeing his narrow-eyed gaze had never left her face, 'that with you knowing so much about women, you'd know that a few tears have been known to melt the hardest of hearts.'

She was standing much too close to him to deliver that taunt and hope to get away with it. In one movement his hands were once more on her shoulders, the strength of his grip telling her she could struggle from now till next

Tuesday fortnight and she would not break his hold.

'What a pity for you that my heart is harder than most,' he said harshly. 'But just in case you feel the urge to try that soulful expression ever again, try to come on with the tears I've no doubt you can turn on like a tap—since you seem to have forgotten what my kisses feel like, I'll give you a refresher so you'll know what to expect should you try any more of your wiles in looking for my Achilles heel. I warn you now, lady, I haven't got one.'

Jemma stared at him. Just his threat that he was about to kiss her was enough to start her heart beating erratically. And fear hit her that if she wasn't careful she might find his threat of that morning had not been an empty one.

'Oh no, please don't,' she pleaded hoarsely.

But she was pleading to deaf ears. In Karn Fellingham's book, she saw too plainly, she had been part way to putting one over on him. He was about to use his master card, was deaf to her pleas, the same way he was not ready to believe in her tears.

'Cut out the theatricals,' he bit into her. 'I gave you fair warning this morning.'

'No!' Jemma gasped, his meaning coming across loud and clear; her protest might just as well have not been made for all the notice he was taking of it.

'Oh, but yes,' he said grittily. 'What I heard about you I heard on good authority, and without my personal knowledge, from what I've heard you find it all too easy to give in—only this time you're going to regret it.'

'Don't!' was all she could find to say, as she began to tremble in fear of what he was going to do to her. It didn't sound as though he meant to stop at just kisses, and that thought alone had her reminding him hurriedly, 'You p-promised you wouldn't touch me if I b-behaved myself.'

'True, I did. But you didn't behave yourself, did you?

On your own admittance you turned on the waterworks to try and soften me up.'

She was defeated by her own lies, and she knew it—knew also that she didn't stand a chance of getting through to him, and at that moment panic hit her, and she began to struggle furiously.

CHAPTER SEVEN

DESPERATELY she strove to get away from him, only to find that to have her fighting with him was what he wanted. To have her passive in his arms when he kissed her wouldn't have suited him at all, she thought, but even while she suspected she would fare better if she didn't fight him, something inside her was telling her not to risk him thinking she was giving in to him.

'Fight away, Jemma,' he encouraged, catching hold of both her flailing arms and anchoring them down to her sides. 'Your eventual submission will be so much more gratifying when it comes.'

And then as she lost her balance as her foot came out and she kicked at him indiscriminately, his arms tightened about her and his mouth came brutally down over hers. And as that hard mouth forced her lips apart, Jemma was receiving first-hand evidence that Karn had no intention of making the experience enjoyable for her.

His hands were ungentle on her as buttons from her shirt flew in all directions, and she had a double fight on her hands to try and keep his seeking lips away from her contours, and to try and cover herself. His mouth found hers again, her body tight up against his, and she felt a roaring in her ears that her strength was giving out, as her efforts to push him away seemed to have no effect, for he moved not an inch.

And then, as had happened before, that time he had kissed her in Christine's flat, the harshness in him lessened. His mouth, firm and steady on her own, became less brutal and Jemma began to feel dizzy at the sudden change in him.

No longer was he forcing her to submit, but he was inviting her to do so, and whether it was because she was too physically exhausted to fight him any more, she couldn't have said. All she was conscious of was that she was no longer trying to get her fists up to pound at him, and as once again his head came down a different strength was entering her body and she was reliving the excitement he had aroused in her before that had told her she couldn't marry Oliver. Of their own accord her lips parted, and she just wasn't thinking any more.

Then from a long way off came Karn's voice, hard and uncompromising, and he was pushing her away. And she was blinking rapidly, her emotions in any sort of order that from loathing and detesting him, she had once more, contrary to her nature, given in to the magic of his kiss.

'I believe I said I'd give you a refresher so you'd know what to expect,' Karn's voice grated. 'You really are a greedy lady, aren't you?' he added insultingly. 'But then we'd already established that you're a pushover.' And at that, the look on his face telling her he had known all the time what he had been about, while she had been like a toy boat tossed into a raging sea, an emotion surfaced in Jemma that topped all others she had gone through in the last ten or twenty minutes. Careless of the consequences, her right hand whipped through the air, aiming a blow that would have rocked him had it landed. Only it didn't land, and Karn's face was livid as his coolness left him.

He caught hold of her wrist, mindless that he might break it, and thundered at her, 'You'd better get to bed before I change my mind about letting you off with just a sample!'

His fury was frightening to see, and the terror of him she had felt earlier in the day threatened to swamp her. She tore her eyes away from him, unable to take the look in his eyes that said she'd better take him seriously. Her in-

voluntary glance to the unfinished washing up was followed
by his, and then as they looked back at each other she saw
his eyes go to the front of her, and it was her turn to follow
his glance. And what she saw had fresh emotions rioting
through her, for her shirt was wide open to the world, her
bra, lacy and not doing a very good job of concealing her,
was disturbed, and lifting her eyes she saw from his expression as his glance rested on the heaving swell of her
breasts that he was not as immune to her as he would have
her suppose. And the control on his temper seemed frailer
than ever as he barked at her:

'For God's sake get out of my sight! I'll finish the bloody
washing up.'

It had been Jemma's intention to have a bath before she
went to bed that night, but nothing would have kept her
downstairs after that.

She had thought that once in bed she would fall instantly
asleep, but that was so much wishful thinking, she realised.
She had been up since six that morning and had seemed to
be on the go ever since, so her body was tired enough, and
Sunday or no, tomorrow she had a feeling that at six o'clock
she would again feel that hand on her shoulder insisting she
get up, but sleep just wouldn't come.

How long she spent in reliving the scene that had taken
place downstairs, she didn't know. But Karn still hadn't
come up when her mind, exhausted with thinking about it,
drifted on to thoughts of Christine and Mark.

Karn was so certain in his belief that Christine was a
thorough bad lot. Oh, if only she could see his face when
they got back and Mark told him he and Crystabella were
engaged. That would be a treat she'd give anything not to
miss. It would make up for all the insults and sneers she'd
had to take from him on her sister's behalf. She pictured
him now, incredulous that he had taken the wrong girl
away with him, and felt exultant that whatever he said or

did between now and the time he dropped her off at Christine's flat, she was still going to have the last triumph. She sobered as the thought struck her that he might come looking for her, remembered again he had once told her that she would regret it if she tried to doublecross him. Wasn't getting even with her part of the reason for being here? He had never said so, but it had rankled with him that she had supposedly accepted that bracelet from Mark after accepting five thousand pounds from him not to see him again. She knew then she was going to ask Christine not to give Karn Fellingham her address should he go seeking it.

She wondered if Mark had had her letter yet. Christine would know about it too by now if he had; he was bound to contact her straight away to see what she made of it. Jemma's thoughts went on and froze. Oh heavens, what if Christine telephoned home, told her parents? She quickly squashed the thought. Christine seldom rang home and in any case she wasn't the impulsive sort like Jemma; she would sit and think it out first—might even be clever enough to put two and two together, might make the connection that her lease had something to do with it. No, she decided, Christine wouldn't be telephoning home, not until she'd had a word with her first anyway. What if Mum and Dad had telephoned her, though? What if Christine had let something slip? Jemma turned over in her bed as though to try and escape from her worrying thoughts, then knew that somehow or other she would have to get in touch with her parents. They would be worried about her anyway if they didn't hear from her. Yet she couldn't write to them, not from Cornwall when they thought she was in London. Somehow or other she would have to get to a telephone box.

There was no hand on her shoulder shaking her roughly awake the next morning, and she awoke to find sunlight streaming through the uncurtained window. She sat up and reached for her watch. Five past eight. Perhaps *he* next door had overslept. Silently she slid out of bed, wrapped her dressing gown around her and cautiously tiptoed to peep round the dividing wall. Karn's bed was empty.

Hardly crediting that he had allowed her to sleep in, she tightened the girdle of the tricel robe so that it couldn't come undone, then gathered up the clothes she was going to wear that day, and with her new jeans hanging over her arm she went through his room and to the top of the stairs. Half way down, the girdle of her robe intact, the overlapping edges of her robe began to slip, and while normally it wouldn't have mattered, it was only a short distance to the bathroom when she would be taking it off anyway, just then she saw Karn was in the kitchen and was standing watching her.

Confusion at the thought that if she took another step her robe would separate giving him an uninterrupted view of her curves beneath her shortie nightie, she stopped to gather the folds around her. But in doing so she caused the jeans over her arm to slip, the bundle of underclothes and the T-shirt under her other arm hampering her, and while she made a grab for her jeans her foot slipped and she knew a brief panic that she was going to go headlong the rest of the way.

Then suddenly there was a wall of rock against her chest as Karn must have moved with lightning speed, because she didn't hit a single stair on her way down but was plucked out of the air to lean winded against him. And there, in the hard safe shelter of his arms, her robe having separated for all her efforts, she felt the warmth of his body hitting her like an inferno through her thin clothing. She felt a physical awareness of Karn then that surmounted anything she had felt for him before, and was shocked by the feeling, the feeling of enjoying the intimacy of his hold, the feeling of a heat springing up in her own body. So staggered was she by it that when his cool voice up above her head asked, 'Are you all right? Did you hurt yourself?' the hot colour caused by fear that he might see what she was feeling and so have his opinion of her endorsed had her snapping:

'Let me go—I don't want you to touch me!'

Instantly she was freed. But she was so shaken by what had happened that she couldn't have looked at him then if her life had depended upon it.

'I should have let you break a limb,' was the caustic reply.

Jemma didn't wait to hear any more, but gathered up her clothes, snatching up the bra that was hanging over the stair rail and stuffing it unceremoniously into her pocket and hastening to the bathroom to close the door and lean weakly against it.

What had happened back there? She could still feel the hardness of him crushing her breasts against him as he had held her while trying to keep his balance. Dear God, was she going mad? Was she the wanton Karn accused her sister of being? She had wanted him to hold her, to kiss her, and more. Leaving the door, she turned on the bath taps, caught sight of her face in his shaving mirror and had to look away from the now pale-faced girl with enormous eyes, unable to meet the crazy thoughts that rattled around in her head, let alone meet her eyes.

She felt calmer after she had bathed and dressed. She had told herself it wasn't physical desire she had felt for him. How could it be?—she hated him. No, it was clear now that what she had felt was the heat of relief on finding herself in the safe harbour of his arms and not spread out on the concrete he was standing on with her head cracked open as so easily could have been the case.

She took longer in the bathroom than she needed, but eventually she had to come out. And it was to see Karn standing stiffly staring out of the window. He turned round and surveyed her pale face impassively, his expression hard and unyielding.

'Let's get one thing straight,' he said with the air of a man who wouldn't tolerate skeletons in his particular cupboard. 'I held on to you just now because you were winded, thought you needed to lean against me. I held you for that reason only. Other men might find your curves delectable, but as far as I'm concerned, Jemma Noakes, as a woman, you leave me cold. And far from *wanting* to touch you, I'd as soon tangle with a man-eating tiger!'

Jemma stood rooted to the spot as his words bit into her. He obviously felt a need to put her straight on that score, and from his tone she could only gather he had no idea what had triggered off her need to tell him she didn't want him to touch her.

'I—I understand,' she stammered.

His eyes flicked over her taut figure, her pale innocent-looking face, and his lips tightened. 'Good,' he said. Then, having got that out of the way, 'I shall be working outside most of the day, you can give me a shout when my meals are ready.'

Jemma's face took on a wooden expression. She wanted to ask him about making a telephone call, but with all the jobs inside waiting to be done he was underlining that he couldn't stand the sight of her, that those inside jobs could wait until he felt better able to put up with her, she just couldn't ask him.

'Have you had breakfast?' she asked stonily.

'I don't want any.'

He really hated her, didn't he? she thought as he slammed out. She even put him off his food. She watched from the kitchen window while he attacked the weed-ridden garden forcefully, cutting into the earth with his spade as if he'd like to be stamping his foot down on her rather than the shoulders of the spade. She didn't want any breakfast either.

She came away from the window; there was plenty she could be getting on with inside the house without standing there trying to discern what demonical thoughts were going through his head. Mark would have her letter by tomorrow at the latest if he hadn't received it already. How much longer after that did Karn intend to keep her here? Surely he couldn't stay away from his business commitments in London for too long? But how long was too long?

She gave up trying to think up the answer to that one and set about tidying up the kitchen. Knowing him, he had left full instructions for his staff to carry on without him, had probably told them not to be surprised if they didn't see him for a month. A month in this place with just him for company! Jemma shuddered. It just didn't bear thinking about.

The kitchen tidy, she made her way upstairs, ignoring Karn's unmade bed and going into her own room. It was a lovely day out, she could wash through the jeans she had worn yesterday and some other odds and ends; they could be drying while she was having a blitz up here. Passing through Karn's room, she saw the shirt he had worn yesterday slung over the back of a chair and wanted to walk by it, in fact did, only to have her conscience pulling her back. Damn him, but it wouldn't hurt her to rinse through his shirt.

Not very pleased to be the possessor of a nagging conscience, she jerked a corner of the shirt, pulling it to her, and as she did so saw a small fragment of paper fall from the breast pocket. Well, she'd have to take it out anyway to have washed it, wouldn't she, she thought, poking her fingers into the pocket to empty out anything else he had in there. She found three other pieces of paper and, her suspicions aroused by what they looked like, she pieced the four fragments together and saw that the cheque she had left on his bed yesterday had been torn across and across as if he had little patience with her, and then shoved into his pocket. He obviously had no intention of letting her pay for the things he had purchased, had no intention at all of paying her cheque into his bank.

Her anger against him came roaring to the surface and after washing out his shirt she wrung it out, imagining beautifully that it was his neck. She wouldn't argue the case with him. In fact she wouldn't speak to him again unless it was strictly necessary. But when this kidnapping was over she would send him a cheque, and watch her bank statements, and if he ripped up the next cheque then she would keep sending him another until he got fed up with receiving them and paid one of them into his account.

She found a piece of cord that would have to do as a washing line, then going round to the back of the cottage she hung her improvised line on to a tree and a drainpipe, hoping the drainpipe would hold when the wet washing strained it. Her washing out, the downstairs tidy, Jemma made herself a mug of coffee. Karn was still hard at it outside and she hoped he was sweating like a bull. Her coffee finished, she rinsed her mug, then made coffee for Karn, took it to the kitchen table and went to the door.

'Coffee!' she called, saw he had heard when he dug his spade into the earth and took his foot from it, then straightened up. She retreated into the kitchen, collected the broom and went upstairs to stay decobwebbing her room until long after he had been in for his coffee and gone out again.

Her room was tidy and fairly presentable but hadn't had the soap and water treatment yet, when she thought she had better leave it and start doing something about Sunday lunch.

At half past one, her stomach protesting at being neglected, Jemma had the meal ready. She debated whether to stick his in the oven while she had hers and then call him in, then reflected perhaps that was taking hostilities a bit too far.

'Lunch!' she called from the doorway, and didn't wait this time to see whether he had heard or not.

He came in as she was straining the potatoes at the sink with the aid of a saucepan lid, and he waited patiently until she had moved out of the way before he took her place and washed his hands.

Unspeaking she placed the two plates of steak, frozen peas and sprouts, boiled potatoes, roast potatoes and Yorkshire pudding down on the table as Karn came and sat down. She saw him lift his eyes from his plate and look at her, and felt enormous satisfaction that she had baffled him. The girl he thought she was wouldn't be able to boil an egg successfully!

'Eat it before it gets cold,' she instructed as her mother had often said to her in the past, forgetting in her rush of having scored a chalk mark that she had decided she wasn't going to speak to him.

'Where did you learn to cook like this?' he asked, his animosity forgotten.

'You haven't tasted it yet,' she said, and began to cut a slice off her steak, knowing that unless something had gone disastrously wrong, the meal should be almost as good as her mother made—after all, it had been her mother who had taught her.

'Your talents appear to be varied and wide,' he said, sampling the roast potato and obviously approving.

Jemma wasn't sure there wasn't a sting in the tail of that remark and looked at him, some of her delight at having scored dwindling. But there was no sardonic look coming her way, so she allowed herself to relax and take his remark at face value. Then she knew he had been referring only to the girl he had personally known and not the terrible things that had been said about Christine, when he went on:

'I'd have thought you'd have collapsed with shock when you saw the state this place was in,' he told her, much to her surprise. 'I thought at the sight of the first spider you'd be begging me to take you back. Then before I can turn round you're getting stuck in, up to your elbows in suds with scant regard to how you look.' His voice had taken on that puzzled note, and she realised they were heading into dangerous territory.

'My hair must look a mess,' she said. 'I really must wash it some time today.'

'Your hair looks fine and you know it,' he said bluntly, and Jemma knew he had safely been headed off from any further speculations about her. 'It was too much to hope you'd forget your vanity for more than twenty-four hours,' he added. Then throwing her a scowling look that didn't match his next comment, 'You know your new hair-style suits you, are you so egotistical that you have to fish for compliments?'

'Compliments from you yet?' Jemma tried for his sardonic look and thought she had managed it rather well, then added cheekily, 'The day I meet with your approval, I'll call out a doctor and have you checked over.'

At the very least she expected a thunderous look for her insolence, not to mention some cutting remark that would shrivel her up. But she was staggered to see a grin he couldn't hold back spread across his features. Shattered, she stared at him, watched the grin disappear but not the remembrance of it. It took years off him, and she was further staggered to find that she liked it when he grinned.

'Your lunch is growing cold,' he mocked, which was all she needed to take her eyes off him and concentrate on her meal.

She hated to think she was changing her opinion of him, but he could be more or less tolerable when he wasn't practising to be horrible. He'd chatted very nearly conversationally to her after the first few opening rounds, she recalled as she went upstairs to renew her mucking out. The enmity that had been stark between them first thing had been buried and Karn had stayed for a further ten minutes' respite when lunch was finished before going back to his gardening and leaving her to get on with the washing up.

The proverb, 'The way to a man's heart is through his stomach' came to her before she ousted it. She didn't want his heart, for goodness' sake, always supposing he had one. And she didn't think that having some food inside him had mellowed him any. No, she was more inclined to think, after stating unequivocally this morning that he would rather get entangled with a man-eating tiger than her and having set her straight on that score, that he was now prepared to try and spend however long it took in some sort of neutral zone. Well, they couldn't go on picking at each other for the rest of their stay, and really, providing Karn didn't make any more nasty remarks about Christine, then she would much rather they both made the best of a bad job. She hated being out of sorts with anyone.

Quite unaware that her own feelings about him had mellowed, she stood on the landing surveying his unmade bed, feeling he would be so exhausted when he came in that if his bed wasn't made, he would just flop down on it as it was.

The bed stripped and then made, she looked at the floor that hadn't seen a broom since Nelson was a boy, and had soon forgotten she had intended to wash down the walls in her own room as she set about cleaning up Karn's room.

By the time she had finished, she was only marginally cleaner than she had been yesterday, and she knew then that with the dusty jobs tackled she was just going to have to wash her hair.

She washed it at the kitchen sink and was just wrapping it up in a towel, wondering if she used her hairbrush to curl it under if it would come out looking anything like the hairdresser had done it with his blow-dryer, when Karn came in. He stood looking at her for some moments. Jemma knew her cheeks were flushed from bending over the sink, and couldn't think of a thing to say. That in itself surprised her, because she was not normally shy.

'I thought I heard you shout tea,' he said, after the seconds had ticked by with neither of them saying anything.

Liar, she wanted to retort, and to her added bewilderment found she had to swallow before she said, 'Is that the time?'

'It's gone five,' said Karn, and went to fill the kettle.

It was he who made the tea while Jemma went into the bathroom and made use of his shaving mirror to help re-create, she hoped, the style the hairdresser had achieved. She came out of the bathroom to find Karn had poured out two cups of tea and was expecting her to sit down and have a break too, seeming to have learnt enough about her by now to know she wouldn't apart from making lunch, spend the rest of the day in idleness.

For once he seemed in an approachable mood. Perhaps he had worked off some of his loathing of her by slamming his spade into the earth. Was now the right time to approach him about making her telephone call? she wondered. And as she saw he had nearly finished his tea and unsure whether he intended to sit for five more minutes or go back to work—not knowing what sort of a mood he would be in the next time he came in—Jemma took a deep breath and brought her question out as casually as she could.

'Er—is there a phone box near here?' Oh dear, those dark brows were coming down in a suspecting frown.

'You're thinking of maybe ringing someone?' he asked, his voice managing to sound more casual than hers. Brilliant deduction, she thought, but held on to the sarcastic comment that would have got her precisely nowhere. 'You wouldn't by any chance be thinking of getting in touch with Mark and pleading with him not to read your letter should he not already have received it? You wouldn't, of course, turn on all the charm and tell him to tear your letter up unread and that you'll explain when you see him?' The casual note had gone from his voice as he ended, his expression taking on that look that said he still didn't trust her an inch.

'I wasn't going to ring Mark,' Jemma protested, only antagonism in the air between them now as any thought of keeping him sweet long enough for her to be allowed to hunt up a telephone box went from her. 'Anyway,' she challenged, 'what's to stop me telling Mark everything when I get back? I've got the lease now and once I tell him that . . .' Her voice tailed off at the grim look that came over Karn's features. She didn't feel so brave now in perpetuating the myth that she was Crystabella, but continued, refusing to be daunted, '. . . that you kidnapped me, made me come away with you, I know he'll believe me.'

'Will he also believe you haven't been to bed with me?' Karn dropped in quietly, deliberately.

Jemma swallowed hard. He had that look on his face she didn't trust. 'But—but I haven't, have I?' she said, knowing she was struggling as the challenge fell from her voice and her words came out huskily.

He stood up, towering over her, then said, oh so very softly, 'Not *yet* you haven't,' and didn't need to say any more as he walked to the door and went through it without adding to what he had already said.

Jemma thought she had been beginning to get an insight into the man, and she shivered as her mind finished what he had left unsaid. Still believing she was Crystabella, Karn was saying that should Mark learn the real truth from her, even if he had to bide his time, then at some time he would exact full retribution from her. He was saying that some time he would make her so much his that Mark wouldn't want her. She paled at the thought, then went ashen as she realised how much worse it would be for her when Karn found out how she had fooled him. Found out that despite all his efforts, Crystabella was now engaged to his nephew. Oh—and he must never be allowed to know where she lived.

With Karn working solidly on outside, Jemma left preparing dinner until as late as she could. She felt there was nothing she wanted to say to him, and anything he had to say she knew she wouldn't like.

Dinner was eaten in silence and she just didn't dare bring up the subject again of the telephone call she wanted to make.

The washing up finished by half past eight, she wondered what she did now. The windows wanted cleaning, but she was feeling rebellious against Karn and his rotten cottage. Every muscle in her body ached. Why should she clean his filthy windows?

He was examining the walls where the plaster had fallen out yesterday and she didn't want to sit in the same room with him, yet she had brought nothing with her to read, had no sewing to do. She remembered the washing she had done earlier that day and had forgotten all about and went outside without a word to collect it, only to come back with the washing in her arms, to find him standing by the door watching for her. Did he think she had it in her mind to run away from him?

She brushed past him, dropping the washing down on the kitchen table and set about folding it neatly. Where would she run to? There was no sign of another house, and the main road was miles and miles away. If only she could drive she wouldn't be above pinching his car, she thought mutinously—stuck here with him and his grim silence for heaven knew how long.

'If you want your shirt ironing, we'll need an iron,' she said, the idea suddenly coming to her that if Karn could be inveigled into taking her into town again, she might yet get away from him. She was getting worried about the threat that hung over her, frightened she might let something slip and he would know she wasn't Crystabella before she was safely back in London. If she could get him to take her into town, even supposing he made her leave her handbag behind, then she was desperate enough to present herself at the police station, tell them she had lost her bag and ask their help to get her home.

'I never asked you to wash my shirt,' Karn told her coldly, as if he resented that she had done this personal service for him.

'You didn't ask me to clean your room either, but I did,' she snapped, wishing she'd got the courage to throw his shirt at his miserable head and take the consequences, all thoughts of trying to get him to take her into town to-morrow vanishing as her temper flared. Ooh, he was impossible! She couldn't bear to be in the same room with him a moment longer.

'I'm going to bed,' she announced angrily.

'Let's hope you wake up sweeter tempered tomorrow,' Karn said nastily, and neatly fielded his shirt as she whacked it at him anyway, before she stamped, regardless of their rickety condition, up the stairs.

She was sure it was only to aggravate her further that he allowed his deep, exceedingly amused laugh to follow her to her room. He was the foul-tempered one, not her.

CHAPTER EIGHT

JEMMA awoke and felt cold. It was still dark outside. She closed her eyes again and went to pull the covers up further around her, then realised with surprise that the bed covers were damp. She patted her hands around them, her ears simultaneously picking up that rain was lashing against the window. And becoming wide awake now she thought, great! That was all she needed. The perishing roof leaked!

Hopping out of bed, she had no hope at all in the pitch darkness of finding out from just which part of the ceiling the water was coming from, then thinking sourly, what the hell, she didn't care if her light did wake up Karn anyway. Why should she be the only one to have her sleep disturbed? She had never wanted to come here in the first place. Jemma fumbled at the wall until her fingers came into contact with the light switch and flicked it down. Immediately light flooded the room and she saw that the rain was coming in in three places.

First of all she moved her suitcases out of harm's way, lifting up the lid to let the water run from it and on to the floor, then, her eyes going back to the ceiling once more, she saw that if she moved her bed about a foot to the right it would escape any more drips. She had just taken hold of the end of it when an irritated voice behind her demanded:

'What's going on?'

She turned her head, her colour coming up beneath her skin as she saw Karn standing there, his black hair ruffled, clad only in pyjama bottoms, his chest broad without spare flesh and naked except for the dark hair that grew there. She turned her head away, all too well aware of her own

scanty covering, knowing Karn must have seen from the
light of the glaring electric bulb the silhouette of her curves
beneath the flimsy material of her nightdress. Her eyes
went frantically in search of her dressing gown, only to see
from its darkened colour as it lay at the foot of her bed
that it was soaked. Her brain froze over, her eyes darting
here and there for some sort of covering.

'Move out of the way,' Karn instructed, and the next
thing she knew, his hands were on her waist, burning her
skin as he edged her to one side to see for himself that she
had been making an attempt to move her bed, and why.
With what looked like an easy movement he hefted her bed
up and against the wall to a dry patch. If he was aware of
her embarrassment in her scanty covering it didn't show
in his features as he felt the bedclothes the way she had
done.

'You can't sleep in that,' he announced matter-of-factly.
'Get into my bed.'

'Your bed!' Jemma exclaimed, forgetting her embarrassment for a moment. 'Where are you going to sleep?'

Karn straightened up from the bed, his mouth taking on
a disagreeable line, then he looked at her, his eyes going
over her, noticing without any change in his expression the
way her breasts were rising and falling agitatedly before
his eyes went to her mouth and then up to her eyes.

'Contrary to your wild belief that I can't wait to have
sex with you,' he told her bluntly, 'you can rest easy that
you won't be disturbed. By the look of it I have my hands
full here.' Then, his irritation really getting the better of
him, he said cuttingly, and unforgivably, she thought, 'Go
and get into my bed. I'll find somewhere to lay my head
that won't have *me* feeling degraded in the morning.'

Jemma didn't wait to hear any more. She stormed into
his room, into his bed, and hoped that when he did find
somewhere to lay his head the roof leaked there too, that he

would be cold, wet and uncomfortable.

Really, his bed was quite nice, she thought as she snuggled down, resting her head on the pillow that had so recently held his. She saw him duck as he lowered his head to come from her room to go downstairs, most likely to get saucepans and bowls to catch the drips, and closed her eyes on the sweet thought, wouldn't it be lovely if he forgot to duck on his way back and sent his head cracking on the lintel.

She had a smile on her face as, bone tired, she went to sleep. She didn't hear Karn come back and pause to look at her, an unreadable look on his face, before his lips tightened and he ducked into her room.

'Jemma!'

Jemma opened her eyes to hear Karn calling her from the bottom of the stairs. 'Yes?' she called back, letting him know she was awake.

'It's eight o'clock. I want to be in town when the shops open.'

'All right,' she called back, forgetting how much she had hated him last night as the realisation came to her that she might yet be able to get away from him.

Because her dressing gown would still be wet, she dressed first and then went downstairs to undress, wash and dress again. The sun was shining brightly, no evidence of last night's torrential downpour other than when she went outside to look for Karn to ask him about breakfast. She saw then he had rigged up a stout line from some flex and sheets and blankets were hanging over it, plus, she noted, her dressing gown had been spread out to dry and was taking up a lot of room so that it would dry more quickly. She decided to ignore Karn's rudeness of last night, and had no intention of asking where he had slept.

'What about breakfast?' she asked, as he walked towards her from the other side of the clothes line.

'We'll have something when we come back. I don't know how long it will take a builder to come out here to fix the roof, so I want to get some felting to make a first aid repair before the rain decides to come back again.'

Jemma felt cheered as she sat beside him in the car. He had made no objection when he had seen her pick up her handbag and bring it with her, and the disgruntled man she had seen last night was nowhere in evidence this morning. Of course she didn't like him any better, but it had been kind of him to find room for her dressing gown on his makeshift clothes line, knowing as he did that she wouldn't want to be without it tonight.

They spent less than an hour in town, and were soon driving back the way they had come with a much less cheerful Jemma sitting beside the driver. It was as though Karn had read every thought that had gone through her mind, she fumed, for never once had he allowed her to be more than a yard from his side.

As he had the last time they had been in town, he had held on to her as they walked through the streets. She had thought that while he was purchasing the roofing felt she might have a chance, had measured the distance from the doorway to the street, had been poised for flight, only to hear him say, 'Come and see what you think, Jemma,' and he had taken her hand to pull her near for all the world as if she was the one who was going to be shinning up on to the roof as soon as they got back.

She was sure she caught him giving her a superior look once they were outside the builders merchants, but before she could give voice to her spleen, he was saying just as though he wasn't a mind-reader, 'You said something about an iron,' and hauled her with him into the electrical wholesalers. Then, that purchase completed, he showed every sign of making tracks back to the car.

'I could do with something to read,' Jemma told him,

trying to delay the moment when she would be shut inside his car with him, her chance of escape gone.

'So could I,' said Karn, and promptly headed her to a nearby newsagents.

Disgruntled by now, Jemma picked a thriller she hadn't read and saw he had already made his choice.

'What's yours?' she couldn't resist as he took her with him to pay for the books. '*How to Win Friends and Influence People?*'

'Would you believe, *How to Handle a Bad-Tempered Woman in Five Easy Lessons*,' he said, with such a charming smile at the assistant that Jemma thought the girl would hold her while he beat her if that was one of the lessons.

Bad-tempered! Her! she thought, as Karn drove through the last village they would see before he turned off miles up the road on to the track that led to the cottage. She'd got enough to make her bad-tempered, she was thinking, when suddenly he brought the car to a halt.

She turned to look at him, her eyes asking the question of why had they stopped. Without saying a word Karn pointed to a spot some distance behind them. Jemma followed his direction and saw he was pointing to a telephone box, and she looked at him again, her eyes shining with the hope that he would let her make her call.

'Who do you want to phone?' he asked, and she dropped her long-lashed lids over her eyes as she prepared to lie to him.

'One of the firms I do some work for,' she said, and knew that he still thought she meant to telephone Mark, when he said:

'All right Jemma Nokes, make your call—I'm sure you won't mind if I come with you.'

Damn him, damn him to hell, Jemma thought as she slammed out of the car and walked back to the phone box, her mind nearly taking off with the rapidity of her thoughts.

He was about to call her bluff and leave her looking stupid when she confessed that there wasn't any firm she had to ring ... Wait a minute, though. She had an appointment for that junior secretary's job this morning, hadn't she?

The box would have been filled with just Karn inside. With her there as well, it was a bit of a tight squeeze. Jemma racked her brains hoping to come up with the telephone number of Holden, Smythe and Partners, but with Karn's leg against her thigh, his broad chest so very close, no number presented itself.

'I shall have to ring Directory Enquiries,' she mumbled, and wished he would go outside when she was forced, by giving the operator the name of the company, to let him know the firm's name. By the time the operator was ready to give her the number, Jemma had raked around her handbag and found pencil and paper to write the number down. Then she was dialling the number and on hearing the rapid pips, was pushing her ten-pence piece into the slot and saying as calmly as she could, knowing she was sounding nowhere as cool, calm and efficient as the last time she had spoken to the voice, 'Th-this is Miss Nokes here.' She was mindful that Karn was listening, so she didn't use the 'Jemma' that would have come more naturally to her lips. 'Would you tell Mr Smythe that I can't make our appointment this morning. Er—I've been called out of town unexpectedly.'

That was all she had time for, because the rapid pips came again, and although she had another ten pence ready, there wasn't, she thought, anything else she wanted to add to that. She put the phone back on its rest and saw Karn was already pushing open the strong door ready to go back to the car. He closed it again when he saw her hesitating.

'Someone else you want to call?' he asked sardonically, his left eyebrow lifting a fraction.

'I—er—— Look,' she said, becoming exasperated, 'just

how long do you intend to keep me prisoner?'

'Getting homesick for the bright lights already?'

That word homesick brought her dearly familiar home in Elvington winging to her. Regardless of Karn Fellingham, or anyone else for that matter, she wasn't having her parents worrying about her if they had been in touch with Christine and she had let something slip. And apart from that they were bound to be disturbed if they hadn't heard from her this week. No, she definitely wasn't having them worrying about her if they hadn't heard from her this week, she decided determinedly, and turned her back on Karn, aware that he had let go of the door and was standing close by watching her. She upended her purse on the small platform, a doggedness about her that anyone who knew her well would know not to argue against. She had two ten-pence pieces and a fifty-pence piece in loose change.

'Have you any change?' she asked tightly, offering him the fifty-pence piece.

Not taking his eyes off her, he felt in his pocket and placed four ten-pence pieces down beside her two, refusing to take the fifty.

'Looks like being a long chat—who are you phoning this time?'

'For your information,' she snapped, her fingers already dialling the code for Elvington, 'my parents expect a letter from me each week, and since I can't write to them for an envelope to show a Cornish postmark without them worrying about me,' she stopped talking while she dialled her parents' number, then continued, 'I'm doing the next best thing.' She stopped talking again as she heard her mother's voice coming over the wires, and was swamped by such a feeling of homesickness that tears came to her eyes, and she had to swallow before she pushed her first ten pence into the box.

'Hello, Mum,' she said. 'It's me—Jemma.'

'Hello, love!' Her mother sounded delighted to hear her. 'We got your letter. How are you settling down?'

'Fine, just fine,' Jemma told her. 'Are you and Dad all right?'

'Oh, we're all right. Your father's not saying much, but I think he's missing his baby.'

'Oh, Mum!' said Jemma softly. 'Give him a big hug from me.'

'I will. How's Christine? Though I don't suppose you've seen anything of her since you're no longer sleeping at her place.'

'No, I haven't,' Jemma said truthfully, relief flooding through her that her parents couldn't have been in touch with her sister, and suddenly conscious of Karn standing beside her. He couldn't hear a word her mother was saying, but he wasn't missing a word of her end of the conversation.

'Have you done anything about getting a job yet?'

'I've got something lined up,' Jemma answered carefully. 'I'll write and tell you all about it. I've just put my last ten p in the box.'

'All right, Jemma. Look after yourself now.'

'I will, Mum,' she replied, and forgot Karn again, her expression full of love for the two dearest people in the world to her as she said, 'and you and Dad.'

Jemma put the phone down, her eyes misty. Home had seemed so close then, her mother's manner more gentle, less matter-of-fact than when she had lived at home. Dad was missing her, and she loved them dearly. Unconsciously she wiped a hand across her damp eyes, then became tinglingly aware that Karn had his eyes on her, a stern look on his face as though he was trying to think what to make of her.

'Your parents are all right?' he queried stiffly.

'Yes,' she answered quietly, and turned hurriedly to get

away from him and his all-assessing gaze in the close con-
fines of the telephone kiosk.

The journey back to the cottage was made without a
word being spoken. From Jemma's point of view she was
recovering from hearing her mother's voice and trying to
think if she had let anything slip. Then, sure she hadn't,
she fell to wondering if Karn's silence was due to the fact
that he had seen another different side to the Jemma Nokes
he knew. Would the girl he thought she was have been concerned lest her parents worried on not hearing from her?
She wasn't bothered what he thought anyway, but she felt
better for having made her call.

Karn got on with making the roof weatherproof as soon
as they reached the cottage, deciding he didn't want breakfast after all. Jemma, busy cleaning the windows at one
point in the morning, looked up to see he had come down
from the roof and was standing staring at her through the
window, a slightly baffled expression on his face. He looked
at her his face unsmiling for a few seconds after he had seen
she had caught him watching her, then having got what he
had come down for, he once more climbed back up to the
roof.

He was uncommunicative when he came in for lunch
and didn't linger after the meal, but seemed anxious to be
outside again.

Around four o'clock Jemma went outside, checked that
the bedclothes were dry and brought them in, using them
as a base to iron the things she had washed yesterday. She
wondered when Karn would finish the roof. He'd been
hammering for hours, each blow sounding as if he was
having a private battle with some devil that was gnawing
at him, but he wasn't letting up any. So much for him
saying he was only going to make a first aid repair. From
the sound of it he was making a thorough job of the whole
of it.

'You look tired,' she said when eventually he came in, while wondering how much sleep he had had last night after she had settled down in his bed. 'Sit down and I'll make you a cup of tea.'

'Trying to soft-soap me, Jemma Nokes?' he asked, and she knew then that for some reason all his own he was filled with aggression, and had been ever since they had come back from town.

Perhaps speaking to her mother had tempered her own aggression, but when as early as this morning before making that phone call she would have been ready to fly at him, in the face of his weariness she didn't bite back, knowing that to do so would have them both saying hard things to each other. Calmly she filled the kettle and put it to boil.

'I'm not trying to soft-soap you, Karn,' she said evenly. 'And I know you're just dying to have a go at me. But if you're looking for a fight, you'll have to find somebody else—I'm not playing.'

His jaw jutted out as he looked at her long and levelly. 'Just who are you, Jemma?' he asked quietly.

'What do you mean?' Oh dear, this could be dangerous. Surely he hadn't found out she wasn't Crystabella? He couldn't have done. Apart from that phone call neither of them had spoken to anyone remotely connected with either of them.

'I've watched you over the past couple of days,' he enlightened her. 'You've cooked, cleaned, all without complaint. Which is the real you?' he asked roughly, 'the tramp who lives in London, or the girl I brought with me to this cheerless place?'

'Don't tell me you're beginning to doubt the information you've gleaned about me from your very reliable sources?' she jeered, not daring to let him have doubts about her at this stage. He'd murder her if ever he found out! 'You've been certain up to now I'm all the things you've heard about me,' she said, forcing herself to be angry, when strangely she just didn't want to argue with him. 'Why wonder about me now? Most people can cook and clean if they have to, and with you all set to make life hell for me if I didn't do everything voluntarily, I just decided the time I spent here would be easier for me if I didn't oppose you every step of the way—You did say you'd take me back as soon as this place was ship-shape,' she reminded him. Then, jibing, 'There, now you know that, you can go back to thinking I'm as heartless as you've thought me all along.'

'I still would,' he rapped, 'had I not heard you speaking on the phone to your mother this morning. There were moments then when you forgot I was there, moments when you were speaking naturally as a girl does to her parent. There was love in your voice then, Jemma Nokes—you couldn't fake that.'

He saw far too much, in her opinion, and Jemma felt herself inwardly shaking. She had no idea how much longer he intended keeping her here, but one thing was for certain, she had to somehow make him believe she was the hard-hearted creature he had originally thought her if she was to survive in one piece. The tea made, she slammed the tea-pot down in front of him, then picked up the sheets and blankets in her arms.

'Didn't know I'd been a student at RADA, did you?' she lied brazenly, and not waiting to see what he made of that, she escaped upstairs to make her bed.

Dusk fell, and with darkness descending Karn was unable to do any more work outside. He hadn't spoken to her since she had left him to pour his own tea, but she was wary of him, knowing his brain hadn't been inactive for the rest of the afternoon. In silence she washed up, imagining the whole while that Karn was looking at her, but not daring to turn her head to find out. She had intended stay-

ing downstairs and reading her book for a while before
going to bed, but with the washing up done, her nerves
stretched, she just knew she couldn't sit in one easy chair
with him in the other. There was so much tension in the
room she felt she could cut it with a knife.

'I'm going to bed,' she announced, and receiving no
reply, did just that, marching stormily up the stairs not
caring a jot whether they collapsed or not. She got into bed,
sleep nowhere near to claiming her, and picked up her book
deciding to read for a couple of hours.

How long she spent trying to get into the plot but reading the same few lines over and over again, she had no
idea. But suddenly her senses were alerted to the door of
the cottage being opened and closed, then after a few
seconds of silence she heard the sound of the car door
being opened, then the engine starting up, and then she
heard it reversing back on to the track.

He's going out! she thought, while unbelieving that he
was going out and leaving her. Thoughts came tumbling in
then. Could she escape? How long would it be before he
came back? Would he be coming back? Where had he
gone?

She counselled herself to stay calm, to think logically.
Oh, he'd be coming back all right, she had learnt that much
about him. It wasn't like Karn to bring her all this way and
then leave her to find her own way home. Could she find
her way to that village where she had made her phone call
before he came back, though? It was pitch black outside
and the track to the main road seemed to go on for miles,
and there were further miles and miles before she would
reach the village.

Despondently she realised she would never make it even
as far as the main road in the darkness of night. It would be
the height of folly to go out there without so much as a
torch to guide her way. She could find herself wandering

about on the moors for hours if she attempted it, she thought, and had to batten down hard on every instinct that urged her to try it anyway.

Perhaps he wouldn't be gone very long, she argued with herself. Perhaps he'd gone to the nearest pub, the way her father did on the rare occasions he was feeling a little fed up with himself. A fine fool she would look trudging along with her suitcases only to bump smack into Karn and be hauled—none to kindly, she suspected—back here.

It must have been an hour later when she heard Karn driving the car back, driving it furiously too with scant regard for the suspension. Well, she only hoped he'd been stopped and breathalised, she thought, mutinying against her own faintheartedness in not attempting to try and get away even if knowing she would never have made it.

She heard the car door crash to, and thought it a blessing they didn't have neighbours; they would surely have been woken up by that thud. Then the outside door was opened with a force that threatened to rattle it off its hinges and Karn was taking the stairs three at a time.

And at that point Jemma began to know a fear far greater than any she had experienced so far; for Karn was through the doorway to her room and was looking at her, the light in his eyes *murderous*—as murderous as she had suspected it would be whenever he found out that she wasn't Crystabella. And as the colour drained from her face, she knew then that the knowledge she had expected him to learn once they were back in London was his already. Karn Fellingham knew, she realised with horror, that she was not and never had been Mark's girl-friend. Knew that she was not and had never been the tenant of the flat he had purchased with the sole intention of using it as bargaining power to get Mark away from the clutches of some avaricious female. He knew, God help her, that she was not Crystabella Nokes.

'*You bitch!*' he spat at her, his whole face contorted with rage as he studied her shrinking away from him as she sat petrified in bed. 'You cunning little bitch! You're no better than your sister, you lying, scheming tramp!'

'Karn, p-please,' she tried to interrupt, her worst suspicions confirmed on that word 'sister', but desperate to try and cool the situation. But to her dismay she found the sound of her voice, instead of calming him, only served to infuriate him further.

'Karn, please,' he mimicked cruelly. 'To think I was nearly taken in by you! My God, you must have been laughing like hell ever since we got here. To think I let you take me in, loathed myself for the rough way I kissed you . . .'

'Karn, I . . .' she tried hurriedly as he left his position by the doorway and started towards her.

'Karn nothing,' he snarled. 'Like your sister you've had more men than I can count on one hand, one more isn't going to make any difference.'

He had reached her, and before she could stop him had taken hold of the bed covers and yanked them away from her trembling form and on to the floor, snaking his foot out to stamp them down when she tried to reach over and pull them back to her.

'We both know I'm not the first man to have seen you naked,' he ground out, his hands going to the buttons of his shirt before he tore it off and stood bare-chested in front of her.

'N-naked?' Jemma whispered, trying not to believe what her senses were telling her was going to happen as she saw his hands begin to undo his trousers.

'You don't think you're going to be wearing that night-dress for much longer, do you?' he grated.

'Karn—Karn, *please*,' she implored, but saw any words

she had to say were going to be wasted, as he said with
sinister intent:

'Your time for laughing is over, *Jemma* Nokes—my turn
has arrived!'

He looked nowhere near to laughing from what she could
make out, but she wasn't going to stay where she was and
wait for him to start. He was too enraged now, she saw,
for anything she had to say to get through to him, and the
moment he made to pounce on her, she was off the bed and
racing for the doorway.

He caught her at the head of the landing, her attempt to
get away only firing the passion of his fury as he laughed
a mirthless laugh.

'The possession of you will be better if you fight me all
the way,' he told her cruelly. 'It will give me the greatest
of pleasure to punish you physically.' And then as she
fought like one demented in his arms, she heard the tearing sound of her nightdress being wrenched from her.

Terror-stricken as she had never been, she tried to cover
herself from his livid gaze. But he forced her hands to her
sides and looked his fill at her naked breasts before picking
her up bodily, kicking and struggling as she was, to throw
her down on his bed.

'Which bed doesn't matter, does it, *Jemma*?' he taunted
savagely. 'The end result will be the same.' And then he
was on the bed beside her, their arms and legs all tangled
up as furiously she fought him.

Then his mouth was coming down over hers and she
was suffocating with panic and the feel of his taking lips.
She felt his hands hard against her breasts and thought she
was going to faint at his careless touch, but she couldn't
allow herself that luxury as she fought not only him but
the mists of grey that were swirling about her. This wasn't
like that other time she had thought he had been going to
rape her. There was going to be no softening in him this

time, no attempt made to make her yield. He *meant* to rape her—she knew it, and was filled with a wild screaming terror.

'Don't do this, Karn!' she cried shrilly when his mouth left hers to seek and find the pinkened tip of her breast. She felt his lips against her and found strength to increase her struggles. His hands going down roughly over her body had her digging her heels into the bed to give her more leverage to force him away from her, but her smooth body touching his only served to inflame him further and he rolled over until he was on top of her, his legs scraping against hers. And she knew at that moment as her strength began to give out, when now she would have welcomed a faint, that she had lost.

Karn took his weight from her, resting himself on the strength of his hands and arms, victory his now that her body lay quiet beneath him, and as his passion-darkened eyes looked into her tear-filled green ones, Jemma made one last plea.

'Please, Karn,' she begged. 'I appeal to everything that's decent in you. Please don't r-rape me!'

He shook his head as though to clear it. 'Rape you?' he echoed, and she knew her plea was wasted when he laughed a harsh unamused laugh. 'Raping is too good for you,' he said cynically, 'and if your appetite matches that of your slut of a sister you'll most likely derive enjoyment from my taking you that I never intended you to have.' He lowered his head and Jemma's tears began to flow.

'Oh, Karn,' she cried, beaten, with just enough strength left to avoid his kiss. 'You're going to hate yourself after this!' She knew it for a fact, he had just said he had loathed himself after kissing her the rough way he had, and this was far far worse.

'I am?' His head came up again as he taunted, 'Don't you believe it. I shall hate myself a hell of a lot more if I leave you unpunished.'

'No!' she contradicted urgently, strength returning to her limbs in this respite, and the knowledge coming to her that very soon she would be fighting him again. 'No!' she repeated. 'Wh-when you realise what you've done, everything that's decent in you will rise up like bile in you, Karn.' She said it with stammering conviction because as she said the words, she realised they were true.

'You've overestimated me, it seems,' he threw back at her, his eyes going to her breasts only centimetres away from the hairs on his chest.

'No, no, I haven't,' she denied frantically, seeing the light in his eyes that the sight of her naked breasts aroused in him. She was hyper-sensitive to her need to get his look away from that part of her that only seemed to further his passion. 'I haven't b-been with a man ever,' she said, and saw she had managed to get through to him if only for a brief while as his head jerked and he transferred his gaze to her face.

'You've never ...' he began, before he discounted what she had said, and a hard derisory look came over his face.

'I'm—I'm a virgin, Karn,' she said, her words choking her.

'Like hell you're a virgin,' he scoffed. 'Just what are you trying to pull now?'

Jemma looked him straight in the eyes, blinking to clear the tears that were marring her vision. 'I'm telling you the truth,' she cried helplessly. 'The truth y-you'll find out if you follow this thing through. I h-have never been with a man physically.'

Her tears fell in earnest then, for she could see he didn't believe her, and as the position she found herself in really came home to her, she turned her head away and great sobs began to rack her body. Here she was, naked with a near-naked man over her, a man who was intent only on wreaking his revenge, and she knew even though she was going to fight him that when morning came she would have left her girlhood behind.

When Karn rolled from her, every sense within her tensed ready to start clawing at him when he began his attack again. Then when nothing happened and she became aware that he had got up from the bed, she turned to her side, bringing her knees up so that all he would see of her was her back. She was oblivious to the fact that she was still sobbing, her shoulders shaking, and jumped as though she had been stung when cool fingers touched her arm.

'It's all right, Jemma.' Unbelievably, though his voice had a ragged sound to it, there was a soothing note there too. But she didn't trust him. 'I'm not going to harm you,' he added. And something in his tone, a hint of sincerity perhaps, she didn't know, had her opening her eyes to see him standing over her, the bottom half of him trouser-clad once more. 'God, I've terrified you, haven't I?' he said, his voice sounding thick in her bewildered ears. Then, sounding more strong, 'Come on, Jemma, back into your own bed. I'll go down and make you a hot drink.'

And before she could open her mouth to tell him to go to hell and that she didn't want him doing anything for her, he had picked her up in his arms and as she turned her sobbing face into his chest, he carried her back into her room and placed her on to the bed, picking up the covers to pull them over her sob-convulsed body.

Jemma cried brokenheartedly at the fright he had given her and didn't hear him go away or come back later bearing a mug of hot, sweet tea. She hated him—God, how she hated him! She hated him with all her heart, hated him with everything that was in her.

And then, while her hate for him was threatening to consume her, to take over all her thoughts and feelings, she heard his voice at the side of her. His voice, not like

Karn's voice as she had heard it so many times, sarcastic, jibing, loathing, but sounding as though he was hating himself far more than she could ever hate him, as he said:

'Don't cry, Jem. Please don't cry.'

Startling then, like something dropping out of the skies, least expected and entirely unwanted, came the knowledge that she didn't hate him. He had terrified her, half scared her to death, had been ready to take his awful revenge, and yet she didn't hate him. She knew then why when left alone in the cottage she had made no attempt to escape. The plain truth hit her that her subconscious had known what she had not—she hadn't wanted to escape; she wanted to be near him. Appallingly, like a bombshell shattering all other thought, she knew at that moment that she loved him, loved him as she would never love anyone else ever.

'I know you can't bear to look at me,' Karn said quietly, while she was in fresh shock at her discovery. 'It will be some time before I can look at myself, believe me. But if I leave your drink here on the floor beside you, will you promise me you'll drink it?'

She wanted to look at him, wanted to see if she still loved him when she saw his face, but nothing would get her face up from the pillows. 'Y-es, I'll d-drink it,' she said, trying to hold her shuddering sobs back.

She heard him move then, thought he had probably gone into the other room, maybe to sleep—who knew?—and fought to get herself under control. She didn't want him returning if her sobbing kept him awake. For herself she thought it was going to be the longest night of her life. Oh, how could she love him when he had been so vile to her?

She remembered his voice the way it had been when, as though it pained him to hear her sobbing, he had said, 'Don't cry, Jem,' and had to fight hard not to break into fresh sobs. She loved that man, and there wasn't a thing she could do about it.

CHAPTER NINE

IF Jemma had been hoping the knowledge that had come to her last night that she loved Karn had been a figment of her imagination to be accredited to her near-hysterical state, as she went down the stairs the next morning, looked briefly in his direction before without a word bolting for the bathroom, and in that brief glance at him, she knew it was not.

She stared at her swollen eyelids in his shaving mirror, remembered all too clearly what had so nearly happened last night, what in his violent anger he had been about to do to her—would have done, it had to be admitted, had she not been able to get through to him—and realised with despair that even had he carried out his intent, she would still have loved him. She turned away from her reflection and set about getting washed and dressed and trying to rid him from her mind. Pointless weaving rosy dreams. In the most unlikely event that Karn returned her feelings, and that just showed how far gone she was to think along those lines, then he would never marry her. A mirthless smile crossed her lips; why was she thinking of marriage? If Karn ever showed himself even remotely interested in her, he would never think of her and marriage in the same sentence. He would want a wife who was above the sort of deceit she had practised on him.

Her eyes bathed, knowing if she spent another hour dabbing at them the swelling wasn't going to go down any more until it was ready, she took her courage in both hands —Karn had to be faced some time—and opened the bathroom door.

'Come and have a cup of tea,' he said, seeing her hovering. Without looking at her again, he poured her a mugful and placed it on the table in front of the chair she usually sat at.

Jemma went to take her seat, her fingers trembling as she reached for her mug.

'Don't be afraid of me, Jemma,' said Karn, as he mistook the reason for her trembling fingers clutching round the heat of the mug. 'I know after what I put you through last night you hate my guts, but you have my word nothing like that will happen again.'

'I'm—I'm not afraid of you,' she said huskily, finding her voice at the self-loathing she heard in his, and loving him, unable to take that he was mentally flailing himself. Bravely she looked up, saw him observing her swollen lids and quickly looked down again, not sure that he believed she wasn't afraid of him, but unable to say more on the subject.

She sipped her tea, the morose silence stretching endlessly between them, the agitation of her feelings growing the longer the silence went on.

'How did you find out?' was jerked from her as the silence got through to her. 'About me not being Crystabella, I mean.' Oh, what had she done but gone and brought the subject up when all she wanted to do was forget it and what it had ignited? Her face went crimson as she recalled Karn tearing her nightdress from her last night, her naked body wrestling under his.

Her tea slopped over when his hand came over hers to stay her restless fingers. She tried to pull her hand away and immediately he took his hand from hers at what he thought was her revulsion at his touch. She looked at him then and saw his face was wearing an expression that could only be called grim.

'Don't flinch from me, Jemma,' he told her tightly. 'I

shan't harm you again,' he added grittily before going on to tell her the answer to her question. 'After you went to bed last night I stayed down here thinking. The girl I'd got to know since we arrived here just didn't tie in with your reputation. And while I was convinced that all the facts I had heard about you were true they just didn't equate. I remembered the call you made to your mother, how anxious you were that your parents shouldn't worry about you, and at that point I decided something was very wrong. I took a drive in the car, needing to be away from—the cottage, to take an objective look at what I *knew* to be true and what I'd *seen* to be true. And then I came to the conclusion that my informants must be wrong.'

'You gave me the benefit of the doubt?' Jemma interrupted him, as surprised, since Karn had never shown any signs of weakening in his opinion of her as much as what he was telling her, that after she had gone to bed he had spent so much time in trying to puzzle her out.

'Yes,' he agreed. 'As I saw it then I'd made a monumental mistake. The only thing I could do to put it right, since you'd as good as told me you were in love with Mark, was to get in touch with him straight away. I thought he should have received your letter and was going to confess the whole of my part in it.'

'Oh,' said Jemma, everything coming clear to her now. No wonder he had been as mad as hell! Mark would have told him he was already engaged to Crystabella, and aside from knowing himself hoodwinked, Karn's fury would boil over at that news alone. 'So you telephoned Mark . . .' she prompted him hesitatingly.

'Yes, I telephoned him, and what a surprise I got!'

'He told you he was engaged to Christine—Crystabella?'

Karn didn't answer her straight away, and she looked at him only to see he was staring away from her a harsh look on his face. Then, turning, he held her look, and said slowly, 'Mark isn't engaged to your sister.'

'Not eng ... But I thought you said he was going to ask her to marry him?'

'He did,' Karn stated shortly. 'He also, as I suggested he should, told your sister his financial situation.' He paused, then added succinctly, 'Mark will not be seeing her again.'

'You mean Christine turned him *down*! But—but I thought she was in love with him,' she said, bewildered.

'So did Mark, poor sap. He's since found out that the only person she loves is herself.'

'Oh no,' said Jemma, not wanting to believe what he was telling her, what he had believed all along that once Christine knew Mark was penniless then she wouldn't want to know him. But Karn, after one look at her shattered face, seemed to want the rest of it said and quickly, and gave her no time to dwell on how the sister she had known and loved had turned into someone she didn't know at all.

'As soon as Mark answered the phone I knew something was wrong, thought he'd received your letter. But before I could begin to put things right he was pouring everything out, how he'd gone to see Crystabella on the Friday you were with me. It didn't take a genius to see that I'd had a fast one pulled on me, and when I had the chance I asked him if he knew of a Jemma Nokes. He told me Jemma was Crystabella's sister—confirming it, if I needed confirmation just who I had with me, by stating you were nothing like her in appearance and had green eyes as opposed to her blue ones. I came away from that phone flaming over the cold way your sister had rejected him, and seeing everything through a red haze over the trick you'd pulled on me. As I saw it then there was nothing to choose between the two of you. Ever since I'd brought you here you'd been laughing up your sleeve, I thought—I don't remember driving back here. All I could think of was of giving you something that would make you laugh on the other side of your face.'

Jemma looked down into the remains of her tea. She had been frightened from the outset that Karn might find out before she got back to London, had been right to be frightened. He had absolutely petrified her last night.

'What I attempted to do to you last night was unforgivable,' Karn said from across the table. 'It seems last night was my night for thinking, and as I lay listening to you trying to stifle your sobbing, I realised that since you have no knowledge of sexual involvement it was no wonder I had you terrified. I realised too that by my coming to the flat the way I did that time, nothing in my attitude very pleasant, it was natural you shouldn't have been very communicative with me. You could have put me right, of course, told me who you really were, but the way I was then, I saw last night that you couldn't help but want to protect your sister if you felt she was being threatened.'

'Christine had told me of the—er—funny phone calls she used to get,' Jemma confessed. 'With you looking so—disagreeable, I thought you might be . . .'

'Some nut trying to do her harm,' Karn put in, seeming not to be offended on recalling how he had been that day.

'You understand then why I . . .' She broke off. If Karn had discovered a girl different from the one he thought she was, then she in turn was learning that he had a nicer side to him too—perhaps she had always known it, perhaps that was why she loved him . . .

He didn't answer her question; perhaps he had already answered it. He'd been equal to thinking everything over and had been more fair in his summing up than she deserved anyway. Then as she looked at him he gave her the first really warm smile he had ever given her, and her heart just flipped right over so that she just had to look away. Then her heart began to beat rapidly when he suggested:

'What do you say to calling a halt to hostilities?' adding, 'Let's have a truce for today, Jemma?'

She had to look at him again; there was no harshness in his voice at all. 'Aren't we going back to London today?' she asked carefully.

'There's still a lot to be done here,' he said, turning his head to look about him. 'I could do with your help.' He paused, his eyes back on her, then asked, 'Do you have to rush back to London?'

Jemma studied her fingernails. Once she was back in London she would never see him again. And although she knew she wasn't doing herself the least bit of good, if there was a chance of just a few extra days in his company, then she knew she just had to have those few extra days.

'I promise you you have no need to be afraid of me,' Karn put in softly when she was a long time answering.

'I've—I've nothing to rush back to London for,' Jemma told him, and was delighted that he looked pleased with her answer.

'Good,' was all he said. Then a conspiratorial look came over his features, lightening his face, making him more dear to her than ever. 'Why don't we play truant today? We've worked hard. Let's take the day off.'

'But I thought you said there was a lot to do here ...' Jemma began, before she caught some of his lightheartedness. 'Why not?' she said. And barely were the words out of her mouth than Karn was suggesting they got in the car and went wherever the fancy took them.

This was pure and utter madness, Jemma thought as up in her room she exchanged her jeans for a pretty cotton frock she had purchased last Friday. But madness or not, she didn't care. Karn had declared today a holiday, and she was going to enjoy every moment of it.

They had lunch in St Ives, and for Jemma that morning was the most wonderful of her whole life. Karn seemed as content as she to enjoy the beautiful scenery, stopping every so often to take it in, seeming content too to have snatched conversations here and there, never once a harsh word creeping in. It was an idyllic time for her, a time she would remember for the rest of her life. Over lunch he drew her out to tell him something of her life in Elvington, observing without her knowing it that she had had a happy childhood, was devoted to her parents, and had a wide circle of friends back in her home town.

After lunch they strolled round St Ives, getting separated every so often by the narrow pavements and holidaymakers, but always Karn would be near, sometimes taking Jemma's arm when her way was blocked by other pedestrians. And when they stopped at one of the many craft shops and she admired a small pottery candle-holder, no more than two inches high, she again got separated from him, only to find he had nipped into the shop and bought the candle-holder for her.

'Oh, Karn, thank you!' she said, her eyes shining with pleasure. For all it was an inexpensive gift she knew she would treasure it all her life.

Eventually they made their way back to the car, and not wanting her lovely day to end, when Karn asked her if there was anywhere in particular she would like to go, she asked:

'Are we very far from Land's End? I've never been there.'

'Then, Cinderella, you shall go to the ball,' said Karn, and she laughed up at him because he was her Prince Charming after all.

Karn had been smiling too, but she thought as he turned his head abruptly away from her upturned smiling face, that his smile had disappeared, and she fretted for a moment that perhaps she might be being too greedy. Perhaps he wanted to get back to the cottage. She almost told him she had changed her mind about wanting to see Land's End, but just then he made some lighthearted observation and all was right with her world again.

Jemma thought Land's End impressive with its giant cliffs and rocks. But it was the gulls circling overhead, their legs tucked back as they suspended themselves in mid-air before swooping away, that she found fantastic. 'I could stay watching them for hours,' she told an indulgent Karn, who made no move to hurry her.

'Feel like stretching your legs?' he asked when she had looked her fill, and she was eager to fall in with anything he suggested.

They strolled through the lush greenery away from other tourists, then when he suggested they sat down and enjoy the sea air, Jemma was equally ready to comply. And when he said, so completely out of character, taking off one of the old T.V. commercials, 'Nice 'ere, 'n it?' laughter bubbled up inside her and wasn't checked as it spilled over, and she fell deeper in love with him than she had thought possible. Through the day he had proved himself to be a witty raconteur. But here he was proving he could be equally at home with the ridiculous as with sophisticated humour.

Then suddenly, when he had been laughing with her, his expression altered and he asked seriously, 'What were you doing at your sister's flat those times I called, Jemma? You don't live with her, do you?'

'No,' she replied, her own laughter fading, wondering since he appeared to know so much about Christine if he also suspected she wouldn't be agreeable to sharing. 'I—er—had something I needed to think over,' she said, knowing he wouldn't be interested in what it was. 'I decided if Christine would have me I would spend my holiday in London.'

'You don't live in London?' he asked, as she had thought,

not at all interested in what she had to think over.

'I do now. I didn't then. But when my holiday was over I'd decided I would like to make a career for myself. Job opportunities in Elvington aren't brilliant,' she explained, 'and I thought London was the place for me.'

'So you've only just moved.'

'About a week ago,' she told him, feeling quite relaxed. 'I found somewhere to live while I was on holiday, then worked my month's notice and moved into my flat. As flats go its nothing to rave over, but with loads of white paint I've been able to make it liveable in.'

It was amazing how well they were getting on together, she thought. It was a pity there would be no Karn in her future, for today they were such easy companions, she just knew they would have fared well together. The thought almost made her cry, and she turned her head away, grasping at anything to say to get her over this moment.

'I did rip that cheque up,' she said. 'You know, that one for five thousand pounds.'

'I believe you,' said Karn, when she had thought he never would, and she wanted to cry again when he said, 'You only said that amount to call my bluff, didn't you?' She nodded, choked that in his thinking he had come up with so many right answers. 'I'll bet you nearly passed out when I left the flat with you holding my cheque,' he teased.

Jemma felt better, and grinned. 'I intended to tear it up in front of you and then stuff it in your top pocket with a few well chosen words. Only you were too fast for me.'

They lapsed into a comfortable silence. Then as Jemma sat gazing out to sea, Karn's voice floated across to her, his voice casual, she thought, but with a touch of interest as he asked the question she had decided he wouldn't.

'Tell me, Jemma, are you going to let me know what it was that had you holidaying in London to think over?'

'Er——' She wasn't sure she wanted to tell him about Oliver. Karn had once told her he didn't kiss and tell, and she thought that marriage proposals fell into the same category. But with everything going so well today, she just couldn't find it in her to be the one to sound the first sour note by refusing to answer him. 'Well, actually,' she said at last, 'I'd been dating someone for about six months, then when he took me home one night, he—er—he asked me to marry him.'

She was aware that Karn had stiffened beside her and couldn't think of any reason why he should do that unless he was jealous of her past boy-friends. Which just showed, she thought, how badly she'd got it. She'd be imagining him in love with her next, and that would be the wildest of her imaginings to date. Perhaps he thought, like her, that marriage proposals were private, that she shouldn't have told him. But he had asked, hadn't he?

'Go on,' he prompted, showing he was not at all averse to her telling him of her proposal of marriage. 'This man asked you to marry him, then what?' There was nothing in his tone but polite interest, and any distant possibility that he might be jealous was firmly put down, but having got this far, Jemma went on.

'Well, I hadn't been expecting him to propose, so I went to London to think about it—needed time to think. Oliver was demanding an answer in a few days and I just didn't know what answer to give him. I didn't know whether I wanted to marry him or not.'

'And you found the answer in London?'

Too late she realised she was on shaky ground. If Karn asked her if anything had happened to help her come to her decision, she didn't at that moment have very much faith in her powers of invention to keep him from knowing that the response she had given him to his kisses was what had happened.

'I was away for almost two weeks,' she said, hanging desperately on to her calm so he shouldn't know her insides were already churning over at the thought of him getting too near to the truth, for she was realising now that as far back as that second meeting with him, something in him had attracted her. 'It was long enough to take an objective view and realise that had I been in love with him, then I wouldn't have had to think about it,' she ended.

With relief she saw Karn appeared to be satisfied with that. He didn't question her further on the subject anyway, thank goodness, and that had her insides settling down again.

'So having decided Oliver wasn't for you, you decided you wanted to make a career for yourself in London?'

'Yes,' said Jemma, feeling happier now. 'As I told you, I'd been decorating my flat. I was sleeping at Christine's to get away from the smell of paint. I had an interview arranged for a job—Holden, Smythe and Partners,' she added, reminding him, 'I rang them yesterday and told them I couldn't make it.'

'Oh, the sins you're laying at my door,' he teased, and saw the edge of a smile tug at her lips. 'Something else will turn up, don't you worry,' he told her confidently. Then he frowned suddenly as he asked, 'Are these your clothes you're wearing or your sister's?'

'Mine, all mine,' said Jemma. 'I'd decided I'd like a new image, so I spent most of that Friday fitting myself out with a new wardrobe. I'd only just popped back to Christine's to transfer my new clothes to one of her suitcases because I was having trouble with the paper carriers, and then you arrived.'

She saw from his look that he was remembering the carriers she had taken down to the dustbin. 'So you were all packed, ready to go,' he commented.

'Except for a dressing gown,' she said, adding tongue in

cheek, 'and of course, working clothes.'

Karn laughed and Jemma laughed with him. Then still in the same light vein Karn was clearing up the only other thing that seemed to be puzzling him and asking her why she had been in tears that night they had begun to do the washing up together.

Jemma looked at him and felt just then so at one with him, especially since he had decided for himself they hadn't been crocodile tears after all, that she was able to tell him, 'My father said I would be rushing home to have my Noddy drinking mug topped up—I was feeling a bit homesick, that's all.'

'Feeling the contrast too great with the way we were from what you were used to,' he said, with that amazing insight of his. 'I wasn't very nice to you, was I?' he added, his face taking on a severe look, which wasn't at all what she wanted.

'Well, nobody can be nice *all* the time,' she said, aiming for an impish note, and was delighted when he threw her a lopsided grin. Then he was helping her to her feet and saying:

'Come on, let's go and hunt up one of those Cornish cream teas.'

'Pig,' said Jemma, thinking it a good idea, for all they had both eaten heartily at lunch time.

'I'll get you for that,' he threatened, and Jemma was happy.

When they returned to the cottage just as dusk was falling, Jemma thought it had been a day she would never forget. Karn seemed to be in excellent spirits and her cup was full and overflowing as they dashed inside the cottage just as the rain that had been threatening for the last hour began to empty down.

Karn's lighthearted mood lasted throughout that evening. He appeared not to want any seriousness to enter their conversation, and she was happy that it should be so. She felt comfortable with him and wanted the day to never end. But of course it had to and when ten o'clock came and went, though not wanting to go to bed, she knew she would feel he had had enough of her that day if he was the one to suggest it was about time they retired for the night.

'I think I'll go up now,' she said, and saw him look at her. She thought she saw regret in that look that a happy day for him too was over, but she discounted that idea, she didn't trust her imagination, and knew she was right not to when Karn said, without a trace of regret in his voice:

'You do that, Jemma. I think I'll stay down and read for a while.'

He could, she supposed, after last night's experience, have been telling her she could sleep soundly in her bed, that she would be asleep by the time he came up and would sleep undisturbed. But she didn't see it that way. The smile left her face and she went up the stairs thinking sourly that he had been wanting to read his wretched book for hours, only he hadn't been able to because she had kept talking.

She only just reached her room when she heard him coming up the stairs after her. Oh lord, had she given herself away? Had he noticed she was put out by the absence of her saying 'Goodnight'? If only she was a better actress!

'Jemma, I ...' Karn said in her doorway, then stopped as, forgetting to duck as he went to come forward, he banged his head against the lintel.

In a second her concern had killed every other thought, and she went dashing over to him, only to trip over her suitcase, see Karn was already recovering from the blow, and he was just in time to move to catch her as she would have gone flying past him and could have landed anywhere. Neither of them had their balance as she catapulted into his arms, and it was no surprise to her when they landed in a heap on her bed.

'Are you all right?' they said together, and both laughed.

Apart from a red mark on his forehead, his head didn't look any worse for wear, she thought as she lay there prior to making an attempt to get out of his arms. Their laughter spurred on an imp of mischief within her, and she said wickedly:

'That bang on the head couldn't have happened to a nicer fellow.'

'Why, you . . .' said Karn, smiling down at her as she lay partly beneath him.

Then, as he looked at her, she saw his smile disappear, saw his eyes go to her mouth, felt his arms tighten about her, and while the thought came to her, he's going to kiss me, she felt herself powerless to do anything to prevent it.

'Jemma,' he said, his voice thick in his throat, and then his head was coming down blotting out the light, blotting out his features, and she closed her eyes as his warm mouth came down over hers in a kiss that was nothing like any other time he had kissed her. This time it was tender, not cruel.

Then Karn lifted his head and smiled down at her, and when she smiled back, the terrified girl she had been last night nowhere in evidence, his head came down once more and he traced gentle kisses across her throat and as far as the neck of her dress would allow.

Like the sun breaking warm from a bleak rain-drenched sky, emotions of longing made themselves felt in Jemma and she wanted his mouth on hers again. And when he transferred his mouth from a spot just behind her ear and trailed a kiss from that spot to the corner of her mouth, her need for his kiss had her turning her head the fraction needed so she could meet his lips.

Subtly, his kisses deepened, lengthened, and her whole body came alive with her need for him. She clutched hold of him, pressing to get nearer, felt his hands caressing her shoulders, going to the buttons of her dress.

'Sweet Jemma,' he breathed softly, and at that point she knew she had no resistance to him whatever he chose to do from that moment on.

'Karn,' she whispered his name in return, and felt the touch of his hands on the nakedness of her shoulders and had to stifle a groan because she wanted him so badly.

She thought he groaned softly as his mouth again met hers, and she clung on to him, giving as he was giving, taking as he was taking.

And then suddenly, in her heightened state, it seemed to her that Karn was fighting her off. And she wanted to die with shame on opening her eyes and seeing him pulling her arms from around him, pushing her away from him as he sat up, his face stern as he just looked at her for what seemed like ageless seconds.

Oh God, she thought, he knows. He knows I love him. And in hot pursuit of that thought came another thought that chilled her to the marrow. The thought that while she had been too far gone to know very much of what she was doing, Karn had kept a very clear head and was at this moment deciding whether or not he wanted to take her, the girl whose sister had all but crucified his nephew.

Then Karn appeared to have come to his decision, for he made a movement as though to take her in his arms again. But he had left it too late. Jemma felt ice cold as she moved away from him, got off the bed and kept her back to him as somehow, her fingers trembling as they were, she managed to straighten her clothes and rebutton her dress.

'That's as far as I go, Karn,' she told him, feeling sick inside to hear herself talk this way, to hear that freezing note in her voice, but knowing she had to kill stone dead any passing desire he had for her. For if he did take her in his arms again, she knew the magic he could work on her would have her yielding to him. 'It would seem,' she added,

not daring to turn round and look at him, 'that your prom-
ises are worthless—You promised this morning that you
wouldn't touch me again.'

'But that was ...' he began. Then as her words, the icy
accusation in her voice stung him as it was meant to, he
paused, and his voice had hardened to a grating harshness
as he left her in no doubt that she meant nothing to him
other than a fleeting desire of the moment, and had been
right to deny him. 'Lady,' he said, and if he had been
stung, his words were lashing her, 'for a girl who wants to
hang on to her virginity, you go *too* damn far!'

Jemma heard him stride from the room, and tears were
streaming down her face as she heard the stairs send up
their creaking protest as he stormed down them.

Karn was in the kitchen when her tricel-clad figure came
down the stairs the following morning. He looked at her
long and hard, his eyes going from her face to the respon-
sive body that had been pressed against him last night.
And as Jemma hesitated, her colour high, he said coldly:

'Get dressed. We're going back to London.'

CHAPTER TEN

JEMMA was glad to get out of the cottage and go to stand by the car as Karn finished loading up the boot. She had washed, changed into her green two-piece and packed, all in record time, but she had not said a word to Karn. She had seen a pot of tea had been made and had poured herself some, but had been so afraid of giving herself away that she had jumped when she turned round to ask if he wanted a cup when she saw he had come to stand close by her. His whole face took on a mask of tightness as he witnessed her start, and after that he had kept his distance from her as he had ferried things out to the car.

Neither of them spoke as Karn negotiated the car along the track, and Jemma wondered if all of the long journey to London was going to be spent in tense silence that was growing more taut by the minute.

She had no idea that Karn wasn't prepared to put up with a mute passenger for hours on end, until he pulled the car up at Bodmin station, and then she wished she had said something, because she didn't want to part from him, not yet, not just yet, because when she did, she knew as sure as night followed day that she would never see him again.

'In view of your car-sickness, I think it better you make the return journey by train,' he told her coolly, and reached for her case from where he had placed it on the back seat.

Jemma got out of the car, striving hard to keep her emotions in check until she was by herself. She recalled clearly the many times Karn had stopped the car yesterday—to admire the views, she had thought—but she realised now, for all they had not motored so many miles, that

172

he had been conscious that she had once told him she got car-sick after a couple of hours of driving. Too late now to tell him she had never been car-sick in her life; he wouldn't appreciate anyway that she had felt nauseous then at the thought of him touching her.

She was glad to feel the spurt of annoyance when he purchased a first class ticket for her and then wouldn't take the money for it. It helped to keep her from making a fool of herself in front of him should her need to cry get out of hand.

'I can pay for my own ticket,' she snapped.

'I brought you here, it's up to me to see that you incur no expenses on my behalf.'

Expenses on his behalf! That quietened her. Aside from the dressing gown, T-shirt and jeans he had already paid for—she wasn't sure now she would be sending him a cheque once their connection had been severed—what about the expense to her heart? Though that had been freely given, she knew she was going to spend months, maybe years, paying for that folly.

Karn saw her to her compartment. He was no more communicative now than he had been since she had come down the stairs that morning. For after placing her case on the rack above where she was going to sit, he stood back, his face unsmiling.

'Farewell, Jemma,' he said shortly. And before she could get the word goodbye to struggle to her lips, he had turned smartly about and had gone from her.

She told herself she wouldn't look to see if he was waiting to watch the train pull out of the station, but a force greater than herself had her going to the window. He wasn't waiting. She saw his straight back, his dark head, saw him striding away out of her line of vision without looking back.

It was early afternoon when the train reached London.

And Jemma preferred not to dwell on the desolation of her thoughts as the train had sped along. Back in the flat she was trying to make look like home, the thought came that Karn didn't even know where she lived, and weak tears spilled from her eyes, because even if he did find out he would never come knocking at her door.

What about this career then, girl? she asked herself when she got up the next morning. More than ever now did she need that career. It would be years before she was ready to think about marriage, and probably not then.

Around mid-morning she went and phoned Holden, Smythe and Partners, hoping against hope they would be prepared to see her. But her enquiry was greeted with a polite but firm, 'Mr Smythe has completed his interviewing now.' It had been a long shot anyway, she consoled herself. They had wanted a career girl, not someone who rang them an hour before she was due to be interviewed to give them the scant information, 'I've been called out of town unexpectedly'.

The day dragged by. Searching through the paper for a job that sounded as good as the one Holden and Smythe had advertised didn't take very long. Nor did the letters she had penned to the two adverts that had said 'apply in own handwriting'.

There was still Christine's suitcase to be returned. Apart from the locations she visited in the British Isles, she might well have another trip abroad planned and could be in need of her case. Jemma had no particular wish to see her sister having reluctantly had to come round to believing all Karn had said about her. But she had had enough of anything that smacked of being even slightly underhand, so although she still had the spare key Christine had given her and could have easily have left the case when Christine was at work, she decided against it.

Suspecting she might be going out for the evening, Jemma made her way to her sister's flat and arrived just before seven. She should be in by now, and if she had a date—well, she didn't intend to stay very long.

'Hello,' said Christine, opening the door in her house-coat, looking as though she was getting ready to go out. 'Where have you been? I expected to see you before this after finding my new lease propped up on my dressing table,' she added, barely giving Jemma time to follow her into the living room. 'How the hell did you manage to pull it off—It was you who left it here, wasn't it? I know Mark had nothing to do with it.'

'You're still seeing Mark?' Jemma asked. Maybe Karn hadn't got it all so very right about her, maybe she'd had a row with Mark and that was why ...

'Good God, no! That overgrown schoolkid led me right up the garden path.'

'How do you mean?' Jemma asked, the small lift to her spirits that Christine wasn't as black as she had been painted dropping away from her.

Christine gave her an impatient look that told her she was far more interested to know what had gone on that had resulted in her having the new lease she coveted than in telling her anything about Mark.

'Oh,' she shrugged, taking the spare key to the flat Jemma handed her and watching as she placed the returned suitcase down by the settee, her sense of intrigue growing, 'he had me believing he was as loaded as his uncle.' Then, going on as though the issue of Mark was out of the way, 'Tell me ...'

But the issue of Mark wasn't out of the way as far as Jemma was concerned. She hadn't wanted to come here, hadn't wanted to see her sister. She believed everything Karn had told her, but found she just didn't want to be-lieve that the sister she so admired had nothing in her but greed. And it seemed important to her then in her love for Karn that when she left Christine's flat she should know everything there was to know.

She ignored Christine's avid, 'Tell me,' and asked, 'Did you see Mark last Friday?'

Christine gave her an exasperated sigh, her curiosity about the lease on fire. But she knew that dogged look on Jemma's face of old and knew she wasn't going to get a thing out of her until she had given her an answer.

'Yes, if you must know, I saw him. He met me from the job I was on and brought me back here. He said he had something to tell me.'

A hard look came over her face as she remembered, and Jemma's stomach tensed and she wished she hadn't probed. But she knew enough about herself to know she wasn't going to back down. And then, still with that hard look, Christine was continuing in that way she had of speaking as if she had forgotten that the other person was there. She didn't look at Jemma at any rate as she repeated:

'He said he had something to tell me—I was flabbergasted when he told me what it was. There was I expecting at any moment that he would present me with the deeds of a flat he'd bought for me,' she missed entirely Jemma's gasp of incredulity as she stared past her reliving the scene, 'God knows I worked hard enough on him for it. Then as nice as you like he's telling me he's flat broke, and before I'd recovered from that he was having the diabolical nerve to ask me to marry him, saying how with both of us looking for somewhere to rent we'd soon find something.' She broke off, her eyes coming back to Jemma's face. 'I soon told him where to go!'

'But I thought you were in love with him?' Jemma said sharply, feeling sick inside at all Christine had said, at all the things Karn had said about her being confirmed. Karn had thought Christine would keep Mark dangling, but she saw that Christine had been too shocked to do that with Mark springing it on her he was broke when she had been expecting him to tell her he had bought a flat for her.

At that point Christine's eyes glittered, and she turned on her, not liking her sharp tone or the accusing look in her eyes. She wasn't being taken to task by anyone, least of all her kid sister!

'I'd let any man think I was in love with him if his assets were right,' she snapped.

'No!' Jemma cried hoarsely, the last remaining scales falling from her eyes.

'Oh, for God's sake grow up,' Christine told her harshly. 'If you're planning to make your way in the big city, you'll have to leave behind those ideals that grew up with you in Elvington. It's dog eat dog here.'

Jemma looked at her. Christine was beautiful on the outside, but what went on inside was ugly—ugly. She didn't believe what she said about dog eat dog either. She'd get on without it.

'I thought you might be needing your case,' she said tonelessly, and turned towards the door.

'You're not going?' Christine protested. 'You haven't told me about the lease—how Karn Fellingham comes to be my landlord—why he . . .'

'Does it matter?' said Jemma, not turning round. 'The important thing to you is that you have a new lease, isn't it?'

Later that night Jemma tried to find excuses for her sister, but there just weren't any. She wondered if Christine had always been like this, but being innocent, she had still been at school when she had left home, she hadn't seen anything in her that wasn't beautiful and good. She went to bed that night knowing she would always be fond of her, you just couldn't cut out years of growing up together just like that, but her affection for her was tinged with a feeling of not liking her at all.

By the time Monday came around Jemma was making every effort to adjust to her new loneliness. She tried to tell herself she was just homesick for her parents, for that feeling of being part of a family. But she gave up making excuses after facing squarely that she was suffering from a loneliness of heart, and there was only one human being on this earth who could cure that.

It had been depressing to have a reply from one of her job applications this morning, thanking her for her interest but telling her the post had been filled internally. Still, she had written after another two this morning, and she still had another letter outstanding from the other company she had written to. She'd be all right when she started work again, she'd make new friends and ... Her thoughts tailed off as a picture of Karn came into her mind. She let him stay, his face would come back the minute she ousted him anyway. She remembered the gulls soaring overhead at Land's End. How fascinated she had been by them, how indulgent Karn had been with her, standing for endless minutes unspeaking, letting her watch her fill. She remembered too the way he had made her laugh ... and broke her heart.

On Tuesday morning she received a letter. But it was not one she had been expecting. She collected it from a pile on a table in the hall and as soon as she saw the firm black handwriting she had seen once before, her knees began to shake. She made it to her own flat, her emotions wildly haywire. The last time she had seen that handwriting had been on a cheque for five thousand pounds.

Slitting the envelope, she extracted the single sheet of paper, then was trembling so badly she just had to sit down and take a calming breath. Then she began to read what Karn had written. And as she came to the end, a strangled gasp escaped her as the implication in his letter hit her.

She read it again, hoping against hope that she had got it all wrong. And then any semblance of calm deserted her, and she was trembling again, though not from the weakness just seeing his handwriting had caused, but trembling now with the fury of outrage that he could have written as he had.

Her temper soaring, she straightway took out her stationery, needed to write her missive once, and once only, and before she had time to think about it, she was storming to the nearest post box to mail it.

An hour after she had posted her letter, Jemma had calmed down sufficiently to begin to think she had acted more than a mite rashly. She then took out the letter she had received and read it through once more.

'Dear Jemma,' she read, 'In Cornwall you said you were interested in a job with prospects. I believe I have the very thing for you. It will mean working in close liaison with me, but from what I know of you I can see no reason why it should not be a success. We should be able to work happily together. I await to hear from you. Karn.'

She dropped the letter into her lap, once again blazingly angry. If it was supposed to be a business letter then why wasn't it typed? And he knew nothing of her office experience—she could be dumber than dumb behind a desk for all he knew. Yet here he was offering her a 'job'. No mention of an interview—well, he'd hardly be likely to be interested in her shorthand speeds, would he? 'Close liaison' with him, he had written. Well, she didn't have to be too bright to figure out what that meant, and a cry of pain left her. She felt mortified, humiliated, and terribly, terribly let down that he must have returned to London and recalled he had desired her that last night in Cornwall, had pushed down any finer feelings that she was Christine's sister—the way he had been ready to that night—and was now offering her a job which, if she accepted, would soon have her *career* mapped out. She was glad she had written as she had; her only regret was that she wouldn't be there to see his face when he read:

'Dear Karn, I was in two minds about answering your letter,' and that was a lie for a start, her temper had been riding so high she hadn't had to think about it at all, 'but thinking of you sitting there watching for every post, I decided it was better to have it said than to leave you in suspense. True enough, I am looking for a job with prospects of advancement. But contrary to your opinion of me, I am just not interested in advancement via the bedroom. Thank you, but no, thanks. Jemma.'

Alternatively throughout that day, she was angry, then apprehensive. And it was when she went to bed that night to lie wakeful and again go over Karn's letter, which by now she knew by heart, that she had a dreadful feeling that in her highly sensitive state where he was concerned, she had made one terrible, enormous mistake. Nothing she knew of Karn had led her to believe he was so hard up for someone to share his bed that he would inveigle her there with persuasions of a job. Her own instinct should have told her he would keep his business and private life completely apart. And the gentleness in him she had witnessed, that certain refinement, should have told her he had never meant his letter to be interpreted with the crudity she had placed on it. And she groaned aloud as she saw that by him writing his letter by hand it had meant he looked on her in a friendly light, and she stifled another groan that once he received her letter any friendly thoughts he had for her would be reduced to dust.

She got up the following morning having slept barely at all, knowing that she had seen and heard the last of Karn. When he read her letter, he would designate it to the nearest waste paper basket, and promptly forget she had ever existed.

But in that belief she couldn't have been more wrong. For not only did she hear from Karn again, but when she went to answer her door shortly before ten that morning, it was to see him standing there. And the letter she had thought would now be reposing in his paper basket was in his hand and he was looking grimmer than she had ever seen him.

Speechlessly she looked at him. He wore a business suit of grey, the jacket of which minimised the breadth of his shoulders not at all. Karn didn't speak either, but pushed his way into her flat, closing the door behind him with an ominous thud. Then, thrusting her letter at her, he said just three words, but there was no mistaking the strength of feeling in them.

'You insolent bitch!' he grated at her.

'Karn, I . . .' she tried, searching for some way to defend herself. Many times she had thought it likely he would murder her, but the fury she saw in him had her believing that this time it might really happen.

'Just *who* do you think you are?' he slammed into her, ignoring that she was struggling for words. 'And what the *hell* do you think I am that I have to solicit for favours through the post?'

'Karn, I . . .' she began again, and was about to say she was sorry and plead for his forgiveness; only then she could see she could beg for his forgiveness, crawl on her knees in abject apology, and he wouldn't forgive her for the insult she had landed him. 'I wr-wrote that letter without thinking,' she said lamely.

'So now you've thought about it,' he snarled, 'and you're going to tell me you didn't mean it. Well, I've got news for you, Miss Nokes. I only have people working for me whom I can trust and who trust me.'

'You mean you trust me in spite of me being related to Christine?' What made her rush in and ask that she didn't know, a need to have some word of kindness from him, she supposed, inwardly despising herself for her weakness in searching for a kind word from him.

'You know damn well I do,' he said aggressively, giving her very little comfort in the way he snapped out the words.

'Karn—Karn, I'm truly sorry I wrote that letter,' she apologised. 'I lay awake most of the night realising I was wrong.' She wished she hadn't said that last bit, but not a muscle moved in his face to say it bothered him that she had had a sleepless night.

His expression still furious, his mouth tight, his eyes flicked round the room, taking in her amateurish efforts at trying to brighten it up with the white paint she had told him of. His eyes came to her mantelpiece and following his glance, she saw his look go past the pottery candle-holder he had bought her in St Ives. Go past and return to fix on the small ornament that had pride of place on her mantelpiece.

And the longer he continued to stare at it, the greater did her feelings of a different sort of disquiet begin to grow. For she had placed the candle-holder there on her return to London, and she just knew that with his shrewd mind it wouldn't pass him by that for a girl who could write in the way she had done yesterday, it was most odd that she still had a reminder of him looking her in the face some twenty-four hours after her letter had been posted.

She was in an agony of wanting to get his mind away from any significance he was putting on his gift being where it was, for if she had been as angry as her letter to him seemed, then wasn't it more than likely that that ornament would fast have found its way into the rubbish bin, the conclusion being that she didn't want any reminder of him and what she thought of him in her flat.

'Er—is the j-job still going?' she asked, an impudent question in the circumstances, she realised, but at least it had his attention coming away from her mantelpiece.

'You mean you are interested after all?' he replied, ignoring her cheek and looking far less furious than he had been. 'Aren't you afraid I might yet try and get you into the bedroom?'

'Oh, Karn,' said Jemma helplessly, 'I've already said I'm sorry about that. I've said I know I was wrong to think you had going to bed with me in mind.'

Briefly his eyes flicked once more to the mantelpiece, almost as if he was reassuring himself that he hadn't imagined the candle-holder was still there, then as his eyes returned to hold hers he shattered her by saying:

'Then you were wrong to apologise.'

'Wr-wrong?' she said hoarsely, her eyes going wide. 'Y-you mean ...'

'I mean,' said Karn, 'that I do have plans for you that do include—er—outside office activities. I hadn't intended to mention them until after we'd got to know one another better. But since ...'

'Oh no!' said Jemma, and it was like a cry from the heart that he should be showing himself to be something she didn't want him to be.

'Oh, Jemma, Jemma,' he sighed, taking a pace to stand close to her. 'Don't look like that. Why must you be so ready to think the worst of me?'

'What should I think? How should I look?' she cried in anguish. 'You come here to tear me off a strip for daring to write to you the way I did, then you wait only until I'm ready to grovel with my apology,' she saw the way his left eyebrow went up at the word 'grovel', for she had never been anywhere near to grovelling in the time he had known her. 'And,' she went on, 'as soon as I've made m-my apology, you tell me you're all the things I s-suggested in my letter.'

'I don't recall telling you any such thing,' he further confused her by saying.

'You said—intimated that it—you did plan to go to bed with me when we g-got to know one another better,' she reminded him.

'Yes, I did,' he agreed. And here his face became so deadly serious as his eyes probed hers that anything she would have butted in with was lost as some sixth sense seemed to be telling her to keep quiet, not to jump to any more conclusions. 'But only after I've put a wedding ring on your finger.'

Jemma wanted to say something, but shock was keeping her throat dry, until at last she managed to choke a gasping, 'Wedding?' Did he mean she should be his mistress? That for the look of the thing he would buy her a plain gold ring to make her feel better?

'Whatever your quaint little mind is coming up with now, Jemma Nokes,' he said evenly, as though reading her thoughts, 'forget it. I'm asking you very sincerely to be my wife.'

'Wife!' she echoed on a whispered squeak. Then, not having any faith in her hearing, 'Did I hear you right? Did you ...'

'Marry me, Jemma,' she heard him say, and she took a step backwards, her co-ordination badly awry, because what she really wanted to do was to take a step, a flying leap, forwards.

Karn came after her and close up took hold of her and gradually, slowly, drew her into his arms, holding her loosely as though afraid she might shy away from him and not wanting her to panic.

'Why?' she choked, her green eyes fixed on his dark ones

as though searching for the truth. 'Why do you want to marry me, Karn?'

'Because, my dearest Jemma,' he said softly, his hold on her tightening as he bent to place a gentle kiss on the corner of her mouth, 'because I love you.'

'Karn!' she exclaimed breathlessly.

'And,' he went on, 'I'm beginning to think that you, dearest Jemma, are in love with me.'

'Oh, Karn,' she whispered, incapable of saying more.

'So will you please hurry up and put me out of my misery, because I've been going slowly out of my mind ever since I discovered what it was about a certain green-eyed girl that's been keeping me awake for night after night.'

From what he was telling her it seemed to her that he had been in the same torment she had been in. But oh, this wonderful thing that was happening to her, she just couldn't believe it—and yet she knew he wasn't lying to her.

'Oh, Karn,' she said, then without reservation, her green eyes shining, she told him, 'I think I must have started to fall in love with you from the very beginning.' At that he pulled her close up to him, and their bodies were touching, the magic only Karn had over her already working so that she was having a job to unscramble her thoughts. 'It was after you kissed me that first time, after I found myself responding the way I did that I knew I could never marry Oliver—I've never felt that way with him—not with anybody.'

If it was possible for Karn to pull her any closer, he did so then, and Jemma, a joy such as she had never known upon her, had to make a conscious effort to think clearly as he asked:

'And now—what now?'

'What now?' she asked, lost.

'You said you started to fall in love with me at the very beginning. What now, Jem? What are your feelings for me now?' The small shake he gave her told her he was growing impatient for her answer.

'I'm yours utterly and completely, Karn,' she told him, her heart singing. 'That night—the night you nearly—the night you found out about me not being Christine. Then afterwards you called me "Jem" as you just did and ... I knew then I was wholly and fully in love with you.'

It was a fairly long speech when he was impatient to lay claim to her lips, but he held himself in check until the words he wanted from her were said, and then there were other uses for her lips than words, and she clung on to him as his mouth parted hers, and she was anything but in control when at last he lifted his head and asked:

'You're going to marry me?'

'Oh, Karn—yes, oh yes!'

She looked at him, her eyes unafraid now of showing what was in her heart, and Karn picked her up and took her with him to one of the easy chairs, and with her on his lap he kissed her again, and tenderly caressed her until she thought she would lose her mind with the headiness of it all.

But at last Karn let some daylight in between their two bodies, the dull flush on his skin complementing the rosy one on hers as he said, 'I don't know about your sanity, Jemma my darling, but mine's a bit hit and miss at the moment.' He then made an attempt to cool things by telling her he had come to see her, barely able to retain his rage when he had read her answer to his letter, and Jemma apologised again, and was kissed once more for her trouble, but this time only a light kiss as Karn fought the desire to start another onslaught that would have things going out of control before they had had a chance to talk.

'I acted without thinking when I wrote that letter,' she confessed, then went on to tell him, 'The last time you kissed me, back at the cottage—well, it looked to me when you sat up and looked at me so sternly as though you were calculating whether you wanted to make love to me or not, bearing in mind I was Christine's sister and what she'd done to Mark, and it all seemed so cold-blooded.'

'Cold-blooded?' he echoed, in a way that let her know the feelings she had aroused in him were far from cold-blooded. 'Oh, Jemma,' he said, stroking her hair, 'you were miles from the truth. I badly wanted you. I was about to take you, then out of nowhere came the realisation that since you didn't seem to know what you were doing, I ought to think for you. I knew by then that I was in love with you. I wanted you to be in love with me in return, but what chance had I got of that, I thought, if come the morning and I had taken you,' and here his hand came down to cup the side of her face as he told her gently. 'The first time for a woman isn't always the flight to paradise it's cracked up to be,' and as her face tinged with pink, he kissed her gently, then continued, 'What if I'd taken you and come the morning you regretted what had happened? It came to me then that instead of gaining your love, I might gain your hate. And then as I looked at you, you looked so delectable, I just had to kiss you once more. But before I could take you in my arms, you were telling me I'd gone far enough.'

This time it was Jemma who did the kissing, and she just had to ask him when it was he had discovered he was in love with her, and he grinned down into her face, his happiness to have her in his arms apparent as he said ruefully:

'I think you began to get to me from about the time you were almost car-sick.'

'Oh,' said Jemma, and something in her tone seemed to alert him that she had a confession to make. For he paused while, impishness mixed with being shamefaced, she told him she had never been car-sick in her life.

'Wretch!' he grinned, when the explanation was out of the way and she had kissed him again, this time in apology before urging him to continue with when had he fallen in love with her.

'It was that awful night when I had half terrified you to death,' he told her, his face now sombre as he remembered how he had been that night. Then, his expression easing, he went on, 'You were getting under my skin before I learned the truth about who you were. So many things just didn't add up. And then that night I just had to be away from you, being near to you all the time was clouding my thinking. So I went out to think and telephoned Mark. I knew after I'd returned you to your bed that I was in love with you. I knew too that I should have taken you home the next day, but I wanted more time with you. Time without lies and deceit. Time to try and get you to care for me. And then the very next night I blew it,' he took time off to smile down at her and add, 'or so I thought. Anyway, I knew then that I could no longer trust myself alone with you, so I decided we'd better leave the cottage, and fast. I didn't even dare to call personally with the offer of a job in case my self-control slipped.'

'So you put it in writing,' Jemma put in, and he nodded.

'I thought if I were to see you in an office environment, with other people around most of the time, then I could go back to square one and start from there.'

'In a way I'm glad I wrote as I did,' said Jemma. And when Karn gave her a questioning look, she had the grace to blush as she added, 'Well, I don't really want to go back to square one.' It seemed natural that Karn should kiss her for her sauce.

'I'll second that,' he said. 'Though I had no intention of proposing to you when I knocked on your door.'

'Why did you?' she asked, heartily glad that he had.

'That candle-holder,' he said, his eyes going to the mantelpiece before returning to her. 'I couldn't take my eyes off it when I saw it,' he told her, then confirming he had made the connection she had previously been terrified he would make, 'If I'd thought of it being anywhere after I'd received your letter, I would have thought you'd have lost no time in whacking it in the dustbin. But no, I could hardly believe my eyes that twenty-four hours after the fierce temper you must have been in, you not only still had it, but it was on display. And then I added to that the thing that's been part way to driving me crazy, that for a girl who hadn't yet joined the ranks of the permissives, why then, even while hating me, did you always respond to my kisses the way you did? You'll never know, darling Jemma, the way my heart was pounding when I decided there was only one way to find out.'

'By asking me to marry you?'

'You did say "Yes", didn't you?' he asked with mock aggression, looking so ready to kiss her into submission that Jemma almost said 'No'.

But she couldn't say it, so she gave him a heartfelt, 'Yes!' and was kissed breathless anyway.

ROMANCE

Variety is the spice of romance

Each month, Mills & Boon publish new romances. New stories about people falling in love. A world of variety in romance – from the best writers in the romantic world. Choose from these titles in May.

NORTHERN MAGIC Janet Dailey
MASQUERADE WITH MUSIC Mary Burchell
BURNING OBSESSION Carole Mortimer
MORNING ROSE Amii Lorin
CHARADE Rebecca Stratton
BLACKMAIL Penny Jordan
VALLEY OF GENTIANS Margaret Rome
THE PRICE OF PARADISE Jane Arbor
WIPE AWAY THE TEARS Patricia Lake
THE NEW OWNER Kay Thorpe
TOO HOT TO HANDLE Sarah Holland
THE MAGIC OF HIS KISS Jessica Steele

On sale where you buy paperbacks. If you require further information or have any difficulty obtaining them, write to: Mills & Boon Reader Service, PO Box 236, Thornton Road, Croydon, Surrey CR9 3RU, England.

Mills & Boon
the rose of romance

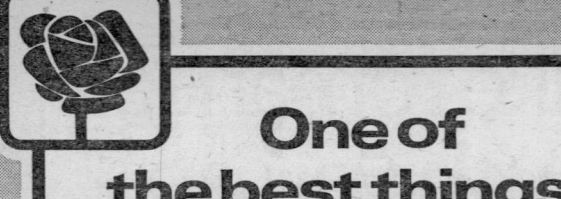

One of the best things in life is ... FREE

We're sure you have enjoyed this Mills & Boon romance. So we'd like you to know about the other titles we offer. A world of variety in romance. From the best authors in the world of romance.

The Mills & Boon Reader Service Catalogue lists all the romances that are currently in stock. So if there are any titles that you cannot obtain or have missed in the past, you can get the romances you want DELIVERED DIRECT to your home.

The Reader Service Catalogue is free. Simply send the coupon – or drop us a line asking for the catalogue.

Post to: Mills & Boon Reader Service, P.O. Box 236, Thornton Road, Croydon, Surrey CR9 3RU, England.
*Please note: READERS IN SOUTH AFRICA please write to: Mills & Boon Ltd., P.O. Box 1872, Johannesburg 2000, S. Africa.

Mills & Boon
the rose of romance